The Prince

A *Charming* Book Three
By: Andi Lawrencovna

Copyright © at Andi Lawrencovna, 2015
All rights reserved. Printed in the United States.
Cover art by Dani Owergoor/SelfPubBookCover.com.
Back Cover Picture from GraphicStock

First Edition:
  ISBN-13: 978-1519378460 (CreateSpace Assigned)
  ISBN-10: 1519378467
  BISAC: Fiction / Fantasy / General

Works by Andi Lawrencovna

The Never Lands Saga
~ *Charming*: A *Charming* Book One ~
~ *The Captain*: A *Charming* Book Two ~
~ *The Prince*: A *Charming* Book Three ~

Short Stories:
~ *The First Ball*: A *Charming* Short Story ~

Coming Soon
~ Rumpelstiltskin: A Shado Novel ~

Acknowledgements

A huge thank you to my family and friends who have supported me throughout the creation of this novel and the others in the series. It really means the world to me to have your enthusiasm to keep me going.

To those writers who I work with and work with me: thank you.

And to M&M, have fun figuring out which one is which, but you've been such great pillars of support for me that I can't not mention you and how grateful I am to have you in my life.

Dedication

To fantasies and fairy tales: Thank you for giving dreams to fly away to.

Table of Contents

Author's Note

Dear Reader,

I do not know where to begin, but I know where the story ends, and at least I have the peace of mind for that. But it is not just this story that I know now, and the Never Lands team with magic and mystery and more deceit and despair than I thought possible in a fairy tale land.

But fairies are myth there too, so perhaps I should have known better than to expect the hearts and sunshine we attribute to our nursery rhymes. The Grimm brothers were perhaps the closest to the truth of fairy tales, and while charming, I do not know that I can say they were happy.

I can hope though, and in the hoping, pray to return to that mythical place, for I might have learned to truth of Cinderella's story, my prince has gone missing, and I do not know where to turn to look for him.

Wish with me, and maybe the stars will bring me home.

Andi

The Prince

"**N**o word yet, though that's to be expected. I've sent the runner back, and the next exchange of soldiers will arrive on the morrow for their turn in the fields."

"Lovely that we could use the excuse of hunting to gather our soldiers and drill with them for a few days." Kit was sure his commander didn't miss the sarcasm in his voice.

"Like you wanted to be out here hunting without your captain with you."

Neither spoke of the fact that said captain never went hunting with them regardless.

"She's likely following whatever trail there is to follow by this point. No other reports of attacks. She must have succeeded at least in her initial assignment."

"The fact that she assigns herself without approval is the issue."

"True enough. I'll let you tell her that, Kit, it'll probably go over better from you." The general sighed, "And technically, I did assign her, my Prince."

Kit snorted, remembering the truth of the man's words, and Kit's own part in not dissuading his captain from going. He snorted because he knew that if he did say aught in disapproval of her actions, she was like as not to skewer him as she was to skewer Marius, though she might regret the deed if it was him, where she probably wouldn't stop at just one blade for his General. "Her temper's gotten better."

"Certainly, my lord." Marius laughed and Kit joined in the small relief, grateful that for a moment they didn't have to think of whatever fight lay before them.

His horse shuffled, and Kit patted the beast's pale neck, promising that they would ride soon enough. The first exchange of soldiers had gone well. The barriers the court magician had erected held strong against any who was not wearing a signet from the court. None could find the camp but Kit and his men. It was a safe place to plan for a war. And it was a sound area to gather an army behind the prying eyes of enemy camps.

"We should get some hunting done. More mouths to feed come sunset tonight."

"True enough, Kit." Marius hauled hard on his reigns, turning his horse about to head for the woods and away from the plateau they found themselves scouting on. "First kill gets to watch the other skin the catch."

"Just the one or them all?"

"All."

"You're on, General. I won't be doing the work tonight."

"Not like last time, you mean?"

The older man urged his horse into a gallop, roaring as he sped away from Kit, signaling the conversation at a close.

Kit watched his friend ride into the tree covered terrain, followed quickly behind. He drew his bow from his shoulder and angled the quiver at his hip for an easier draw as his horse flew over the ground trying to catch its partner. He whooped when he overtook Marius and the hunt was on.

ଔଞ

"Go on, Marius. It's not like I'm in any danger here. We've got patrols everywhere." He smiled at his commander. "These trails have been my home for years now."

"Your idea of home and mine are very different, Kit."

Kit laughed at the other man's words, enjoying the cool breeze against his sun warmed face. He looked forward to these hunting excursions, the few days of the year when he was allowed outside of the palace walls, beyond the bounds of petitioners and commoners and nobles. Even if his solitude was intruded upon by soldiers preparing for war, he still appreciated the beauty of the forest around him, appreciated being a soldier, or a hunter, or something other than a prince, even if his military theory was what led men to listen to him when planning for the eventual attack. He was simply a man here, a soldier preparing to survive, hoping to survive, and this was just land. That no one had ever attacked him in the woods hadn't escaped his notice. Whether it was religion that disallowed the Dienobolos from attacking within their homeland, or if they thought it an unfair advantage to kill him in their forests, he'd never feared them here within their world.

He wished Eli was able to share that with him, but her exile was his fault, he regretted the cause, but not that she was with him because of it. Keeping her from the woods kept her with him for a while longer, and he didn't regret that.

Four men dead by her hand. Four hundred years as recompense. She'd saved his life at the cost of her peoples.

He loved her for more than that.

But she wasn't here, and he couldn't afford the distraction of wondering after her, not even when he felt relatively safe within her once homeland.

Besides, there was a bet to collect on, and other concerns to consider that took precedence.

"That rabbit won't skin itself, General. Get ye to work."

Rabbit stew would feed two, three men at most. The deer would provide good venison for many more. But Marius' triumph in the hunt didn't negate his loss in the bet.

Stew and steak for the evening meal. It would all be eaten that night, unless others had met with success in the woods that day as well.

The stew was a particular favorite of Kit's. He was already looking forward to the meal, especially as he wasn't preparing it himself. He could well imagine the smell of the rich broth set to boiling on the fire. The scent was in the air.

"Stop salivating. I'm liable to spit in the pot just to irk you."

A grumbling Marius was nothing new, and Kit smiled over at his companion. He pulled the ropes with their dangling meat from his saddle, tossing the rodents to the general who drew his horse to a halt, waiting to catch. The man held Kit's stare, his gaze firmly saying what he thought of Kit's need to go off alone, bet or not, safety or not.

"I just need a moment to myself, Marius. There are enough people within calling distance if I should need anyone. Just a moment alone, and I'll be back."

His mother would frown at Kit's insistence to disregard his guardian's remarks. *As prince, you are a model for your people. If you refuse to follow a command, why should they? You must be beyond the mundane desires of the gentry, even the no-blemen. You are prince and must always accede to the wisdom granted you, even by another's decisions.*

Yes, he was a prince, but his mother died before she could talk about the rigors of war or the isolation of nobility. He loved her, knew his father loved her, but his mother had taken being queen much more seriously than his father had, at least while she was alive. Kit missed her, but he missed the childhood he'd been told not to expect.

If he had children with Eli—

Best not to think thoughts like that.

He gripped the reins in his hands a little tighter.

He'd managed not to touch the ring at his throat, not to draw attention to it. Marius would have a fit if he saw it. Marius would know who it was for.

No. Best not to think of that.

"I'll have them save you some stew then, yes?"

Kit laughed, knowing the soldier who had spent his youth training Kit, was Kit's closet friend besides the woman not given entry into the wood, would give Kit a moment because Marius was always looking out for him and what Kit needed.

A moment was a need.

"Thank you, my friend. If I miss out, it's my own fault. If one refuses to be on time for good stew, then he doesn't deserve the reward of a bowl."

Marius laughed, hunching over his pommel while he turned his head to meet Kit's gaze. It was not that amusing as a comment, and both men knew better than to truly seek humor in their situations. The general sobered. "Your word?"

Kit ignored the hesitation in the man's voice, the concern. "My word. No ill will if you eat up my hard won spoils without me."

The general did not ask again, did not require Kit to promise to be careful. The attempted levity was promise enough. "I'll hold you to that."

The stolid response made Kit's lips curl, a half-smile not worn for court pressing his mouth.

The commander wheeled his horse around, preparing to return back to their campsite. He would halt the raising of the protective spells around their encampment until Kit returned. "Don't be too long. You won't enjoy me coming to find you."

"Don't lie, Marius. You'd send the others while you stayed warm and full with my rabbit."

"Probably true. Don't go far. The elves aren't on the attack yet, but once they learn about the mercenaries, that might change. Best to keep your eyes open."

"Yes, sir." Kit saluted the man, mock formality aside, he honored the words and the intent behind them. Marius only wanted Kit's safety. Kit understood that. "I'll hunt out any trouble."

"Don't you dare, Kit."

He smiled at the other man, "I definitely meant to think about saying *won't* hunt out trouble."

"Amusing. I should beat you."

"You can either have rabbit stew, or put me on the list for disciplinary actions, but you can't have both."

"You can be a real prick sometimes, Kit."

"Blame my father, I learned from him."

"It's not your father you remind me of."

Kit pretended not to hear the comment or react to the image of his captain that it conjured.

With a kick, knowing the commander wasn't waiting for a response, Kit pushed his horse into a hard gallop, pulling away from the camp and the soldiers settled down within the space. He bent low over the horse's neck, urging Oberon faster, feeling the bunch and release of muscles as his mount ran free across the open valley surrounding by forest on all sides.

It was a wonderful space, nothing manmade or stone entombed within the woods or their lands. Here the dells were of untended grass rather than rows of crops set to feed a people.

Whatever the elves ate, they didn't farm the land to do it. These fields had never been touched by farmers' hands. And it was a blessing that Kit wouldn't deny, and his heart took full advantage of. The more he hunted the deep forest paths, the more he questioned what Eli had been thinking to ever risk leaving them behind.

Breath ragged, both man and beast, they slowed at the edge of a stream, just inside the border or wood and glade. Oberon knew these paths after the many years of carrying Kit through the trees. He had no trouble following the water to more spacious pools with their crisp water to drink. Kit dismounted and left his horse graze while he washed his face in the cool stream.

Oberon's hesitation to drink drew his gaze to the water, the hint of red tinting the trickling flow. He cupped a handful and raised the offering to his nose, sniffing at the iron scented liquid in his hand. There was blood coming from somewhere upstream, perhaps an injured animal, gods forbid it be a human or elf.

He should not look alone.

And yet he rose regardless, inching along the bank, hoping that he spotted whatever was hiding before it or they spotted him.

The male faced away from Kit, though the five others with him were hardened men, each with blood still wet upon their faces, black clothes meant to help them hide in the trees as they sought out the prince and his men.

"We get the prince. We gut the prince. The walls fall, and our lord takes command. It is a simple enough order to obey."

Was it possible they hid from the elves as well? Did the woodland folk not care that even more peoples were inhabiting their domain than normal? Had they finally chosen a side in this war that was coming?

"This guttersnipe didn't tell us nothing 'bout where the prince is."

The man who responded had only one good eye, the other carved away by a scar reaching from hairline to lip. He sharpened a curved blade in his lap, ignoring the body strung up in a tree and the man who still played with the corpse. "Well you shouldn't have killed him then until he did."

"He said ill about my mother."

"Your mother was a cantankerous whore who deserved all the ill names piled upon her."

"Well yeah, but no one else but me's allowed to say that."

This area was supposed to be clear of the mercenaries. Kit's patrols went through this area every morning and ensured that it was so.

He racked his memory trying to recall a patrol not returned, a soldier lost and not back at the camp. Had he miscounted before the raising of the wards one night? Was he so poor a leader as to have lost one of his own men?

Had he sent men out to die and not even noticed they didn't return?

Oberon grunted and kicked at the ground.

The mercenaries rose as one, turned to the stream and the bushes that hid Kit, that blocked the sight of the horse but not the beast's sounds. The torturer turned the quickest, his eyes glowed in the dark, a mad light in their depths, no humanity left within him. He wiped his blade along his leg, the red smear standing stark against his pants for a moment before the blood soaked into his clothes.

Kit held his breath, didn't dare make a move.

The brute stepped closer. Wind stroked over the leaves, blew them across Kit's face. His bow was strapped to his saddle horn. His sword likewise with his horse. The knife at his side would not do much to protect him from the four advancing towards him.

"KIT! Run!"

An arrow whizzed past his face, finding its mark with a wet thump in a mercenary behind him.

He did not hesitate to obey the command, taking the distraction and his savior's aid to fling himself away from the enemy and towards his horse. Kit managed to vault into the saddle, kicking Oberon into the deeper woods and towards the camp where his men could take the bastards chasing him and he could reach safety.

Damnit. He should have been more careful.

A trio of his guardsmen fell in around him, close on his tail as they raced through the forests.

"They're hunting the prince." Kit knew better than to name himself as the target. His men would as well. He did not think the bastards giving chase knew his face, or at least prayed that they didn't. Luck tended to be a fickle bitch.

Rinauld motioned to split up; Kit following him while the other two went in the opposite direction. Yes, best not to head towards the camp lest it become compromised.

Get out of the woods. Get Kit out of the woods.

But men had already died for him, and the thought of fleeing sat uneasy in his stomach.

Not that the choice was going to matter.

He heard the arrow whizzing before the pain punched through his shoulder. The agony was not instant like Kit thought it would be. He managed to turn his head down and stare at the arrowhead that had punched to his chest, even raised his right hand to touch the blood coated metal tip before the burn began and he had to hunch over his horse, praying he didn't fall from his seat. His left arm was numb. The bow he'd been holding fell from his fingers and he heard the crunch a few moments later as following hoofs broke the wood apart. His horse was slowing, and the world was blinking around him.

Rinauld looked back, nearly turned to come to his aid.

"Ride, you bastard! Get the fuck to safety!" Kit managed to yell the command even as he was overtaken by the bandits. If they knew he was the prince, he was dead anyways. If they thought he was just another soldier, if they thought that, perhaps, Rinauld had gotten away and Kit would know to where, he might live another day. He hadn't seen the body of the poor sod they'd killed. Kit was intelligent enough to know that it couldn't have been pretty if the man was dead, but he, Kit, wouldn't die.

The conviction would have sounded better to his ears if the world wasn't going gray and the ground wasn't rising up to meet him.

He hit the earth and could only think that he was lucky Oberon didn't trample him, that the other horses milling around didn't trample him as his consciousness fled and he was lost to sense.

He woke to the feel of hard wood beneath him, jumbled by the rough turn of wagon wheels over uneven terrain. Kit managed to keep his eyes closed, listening carefully to the sounds around him, counting the different breathing patters of three men, no doubt a driver somewhere up ahead. His arm was on fire, the numbness having worn away to prove that the nerves in his flesh hadn't been destroyed.

He cracked his eyes open enough to look at his surroundings. The small cart boated barely enough seating room for the four of them sharing the space. It was covered, which he didn't know if that was a plus or not given the number of men around him and the condition he was in. If the damn space had been left open, he would have had a better chance of tossing one of his opponents over the side, but he would fight on. The one nearest him had a knife. If he was quick enough, he could grab and kill the bastard before the others knew what was going on. The entire idea that he might be quick enough was a sham. With his arm as bad off as it was, already wheezing with the pain, Kit knew he was no match, but he wasn't going to go to his torture without at least taking one of them with him.

As far as decisions went, it was not his wisest. It was not his worst either, which was the sadder truth.

The cart lurched.

He threw himself to the side at the first guard.

Pain rampaged through his body. He grit his teeth when his good hand closed around the hilt of the knife and he managed to pry it free of his opponent's grip.

A pair of arms circled him from behind, locked beneath his jaw and around his head.

His air grew short.

Kit plunged the knife down.

At least one of them was dead with him.

Two

W ood popped in a fireplace. It might have been a grate
for all Kit knew, but he could smell the charring, the
almost homey scent of warm fall afternoons curled in
the den after a long court session with his father. A glass of
brandy at his side, a book on his lap, papers ruffling in the heat
of the room. Even the quiet of his library was undisturbed but
for the hiss and sizzle of the flame. Soon Eli would come to join
him, as she always did, bringing with her a snack, remembering
his luncheon even when he forgot, was too busy for it. She'd
wait till the king left before coming. He'd even share whatever
morsel she brought

His lip quirked at the thought as he reached to the side
table for his glass of amber salvation.

The fire burned through his body, eating at his flesh rather than the wood.

Kit's eye opened, memory surging in, panic and pain quick to follow. The arrow in his shoulder. The attack of the kidnappers, torturers more like. He pulled on his wrists, biting his lip at the agony of his pierced flesh, the drag of rope against his skin. At least the arrow had been removed, though he wasn't sure that was a mercy yet. Unlikely, given the circumstances.

He yanked at his right arm, hoping brute strength would accomplish his freedom when he could feel the strength of the rope used to bind him, the lack of slack for movement, the tear of his skin around the harsh weave of his bindings. His legs too were tied, boots gone so that his ankles felt the burn same as his wrists while he struggled.

"You're awake. How marvelous. I don't particularly enjoy having to wake up my dear guests. I do find a water bath to be refreshing, but the odor of mildewed flesh and cloth becomes quite intolerable after a time, don't you think?"

It took everything he had not to thrash in his chair, not to turn and try and pinpoint where the voice was coming from, scream out at having been caught in the first place. He panted there, in his seat, waiting for the inevitable, unwilling to hasten the moment of its arrival by searching for the male coming near him. Teeth grit, he replied in the same tepid, congenial tone of his presumed torturer: "I apologize for my rudeness, but it seems I am quite unable to rise."

The bastard laughed, a courtier's laugh, fake and pleasant and hiding the demon beneath. "You are too kind, my dear man, but do not worry over your inabilities. I assure you, they will not matter long." Wood scraped over hard stone. "Before we begin," a small man, glasses perched atop his nose, eyes smiling as he stared down at Kit, cheeks a merry red as though he were glad to be at his task, set a chair in front of Kit's.

Kit's grip tightened on the armrests as the man took a seat before him, legs bent to cross the left over the right, arms loosely folded in his lap.

"Could I interest you in a drink? Water perhaps? Or I believe I can rustle up a good liquor if you prefer? I do so believe that these sorts of matters require at least the basics of etiquette to remain civil lest we revert to our baser instincts and accomplish nothing at our task."

"Civil? I'm not sure I understand your meaning, sir."

"Yes. Exactly; precisely so. Sir. We shall keep to etiquette and thus proceed accordingly."

"Proceed at what?" Honestly, if the bastard wouldn't say it, Kit would. The male was playing with him and Kit found he would prefer knives or whips or whatnot than this charade presented as normality.

"Why, I should very much like to know where his Royal Highness, Christophe de L'Avigne is hiding. Would you be so kind as to tell me where I might find him?"

"I imagine his palace is a good start."

The male tsked, his smile slipping for a moment and a hard glint coming to his eye. The glasses slipped and beneath the frame was revealed the demon eating away at the soul of the man, if there had ever been a soul to begin with.

Ah gods, if Kit believed, now was the time to pray.

"My dear man, the Prince has been hunting for the past weeks as is his yearly wont to do. He has yet to return home. We know this, as we have managed to close all highways to his escape from these lovely woods. His hidey hole has yet to be discovered, and as such, we know he is here. You," the male leaned forward, slapping Kit's thigh as though long acquaintances reunited over old tales, "were a member of my good lord's party, and privy to his location."

"I was not."

"You would begin your lies already?"

The fingers dug into his flesh, all that separated the man's nails from Kit's skin a layer of buckskin too thin in Kit's opinion.

Civility is for kings and pawns. There are times that a prince must not be civil to defend his people.

His mother had taught him that too.

He doubted this was what she had had in mind during that lesson.

Kit managed his best court smile, the one that dared those who desired a dance to come and ask a barely leashed male riding the killing edge. He was feared on a battlefield, vengeance and control. His control was fraying, and he had no other way to attack bound as he was. "Fuck you." He was cordial, in his response, holding the man's gaze, refraining from spitting on the little shit.

The cherub sat back, the smile slipping from his face entirely, eyes going dead not even pretending at congeniality any longer. "I had hoped we could avoid profanity."

"I apologize for having given you the impression that I was a gentleman."

"How kind of you to correct my assumption."

"Indeed."

Kit flinched when the man drew a knife from beneath his coat sleeve, flinched, but did not look away, daring the bastard to put the blade to use.

The steel glinted in the faint flickering of the fire somewhere behind Kit's shoulder. He watched the man nod to someone at his back, though the inquisitor remained focused on Kit. There was a rustling of metal, a crash and sizzle and screech. His interrogator leaned forward, lowered himself slowly to his knees between Kit's bound legs. He touched the hem of Kit's breeches, slipped the tip of the blade between skin and cloth, and cut. Kit's pants parted easily beneath the edge of the knife, slit from ankle to knee, knee to pelvis, the process repeated on the other leg. Hands followed the revealed trail of flesh, catching Kit's breath in his throat. The cloth was pushed off his legs. The knife returned and Kit held his breath as the inseam of his pants was cut to his waist on either side of his groin, baring him fully to the man's view but for his underclothes. Those, the man left for a moment, moving to Kit's shirt, sleeves then torso so it too could be removed.

"Yes, quite nice." A slap against Kit's stomach, barely a tap but enough that had Kit's held breath expelled in a rush, a growl rising in its place, and the male laughed before pressing the knife to the covered jewels protected by small cloths. "Shall we see what a soldier keeps under his clothes, boys?"

Kit turned his gaze to the wall over the man's head, letting the ass do as he would, calming his breathing, internalizing the ache from his shoulder, the pain that would no doubt follow soon enough.

They didn't know they had their prize.

He just had to stay alive until his men found him.

Give enough to entice them into keeping his heart beating one day more.

The knife nicked his groin. He bit the inside of his cheek to keep from making a sound.

"Impressive, even when flaccid. Lovely boys, don't you think?"

A muted murmur of assent was the response to the man's question. So they weren't all male-lovers then. Kit didn't think that would save him much if they turned his body against him. Damn. The nervous laughter tickled the back of his throat, threatened to release. He'd spent a life alone hoping for the chance to sleep with one woman, obeyed the godsdamned protocol that a prince was supposed to adhere to, never touch, never taste, and this was how it was going to end for him, never knowing her embrace, not even a kiss.

One of the kidnappers stepped around the side of his chair, handed the gentleman a whip, and stepped back out of sight. The turning of metal over in the fire grate sounded harsh in the room.

"Do forgive me, my good man. I did not catch your name."

Kit didn't respond.

A pink tongue slipped between the man's lips, wetting the red flesh. He breathed in, whistling at Kit's silence. "It is a simple question." He ran the whip between his hands, shaking his head at the feel, snapping his fingers for the guard to return and bring with him a pair of heavy gloves, hold the whip while the inquisitor covered his delicate flesh.

Kit watched, fingers tensing on the arms of the chair.

"Much better. Ah yes, your name. What is it?"

"Go to hell."

The pain was not what he had imagined, searing as it streaked across his chest and upper thigh, a thin line that radiated agony that faded quickly enough into gentle throbbing. The first strike hadn't broken skin.

It was worse than the strike of a blade on a battlefield. He knew what that wound felt like.

"Would you like to try again?"

"Cousar du pouwn liqfiat."

The last curse had barely fallen from his lips before the whip slashed twice in quick succession, a line down his right side, the second across his abdomen, layering along his elbows.

Eli had taught him that one night when her guards came to rouse her for evening patrols and he'd nearly been caught in her room. *You are pig shit.*

"I do not speak the woodland tongue, boy, but I am quite sure that *that* was no name you just spoke."

Kit's lack of response resulted in an equally brutal assault of the whip, still not breaking skin, still a painful agony he'd not known before in his life. The fifth mark wrapped over his shoulder, slashed across the open wound of the arrow's piercing. It brought a shrill cry to Kit's lips, barely held back.

The man pulled a kerchief from his breast pocket, wiped his dry brow and let the slip of cloth drop to the floor. Kit followed its descent, missed the raising of the man's arm, the ensuing strike unanticipated, all the harsher because of it. This time his torturer did not stop at five strikes or at marking Kit's flesh in red lines. Blood blossomed across his chest, ran in rivulets down the ridges of his abdominals, quickly joined by more lines as the beating continued, grew fiercer. Kit lost count around twenty-two, tipped his head back as the leather strap came closer and closer to his face, wrapping his neck on occasion but never striking his cheeks or eyes or cock. The man was an expert in wielding the weapon, a true master of his trade. That did not make the bearing of the abuse easier, and told only that Kit's agony would last for a long time.

Every third strike, the man asked for Kit's name. And Kit held his tongue, teeth clenched against even a scream at his abuse.

"What is your name!"

The whip slashed a line from his wounded shoulder across the meat of his stomach to the head of his prick.

Kit screamed with the wound, the blood painting his body red now.

"Kit. Kit…kitkitkiii—"

He gasped out his name, sobbed it really, ashamed he could not withstand more than he already had.

He sat in his chair shaking, hunched forward as far as he could, trying to protect his abused body from any more.

"That wasn't so hard."

The man was out of breath, which was at least a small victory for Kit, knowing he had made the male work for Kit's response.

"See what being reasonable can bring?"

The rope binding his right wrist was released, the snick of a knife cutting through the cord, thumping boots moving to his left side. There were at least three men in this stone walled prison room. If he managed to pull the one freeing him over his body as protection, he might manage to take out the other guard and leave him facing just his tormentor and the whip which he was determined to withstand now.

The knife appeared at his left side. Kit moved fast enough to relieve the male of his weapon, claim it as his own. He forgot his legs were bound as well. If his ankles were free he might have managed to free himself, but his ankles were bound and he fell over the body he pulled over his shoulder, the chair fell on top of him, and the whip master laughed while Kit struggled to breathe at the agony filling him. He refused to release the knife in his hand. Lying prone on the ground, his arm outstretched before him, the male on top of him stood and stepped on his right shoulder. There was a pop and then there was pain and Kit's fingers spasmed their grip on the blade before releasing, both arms useless now, one dislocated, the other unhealed from the arrow of a day before.

"Get him back in the chair. And get it ready."

Kit yelled and he thrashed and he screamed and he fought and it was all useless as they bound him back to his seat, lacing ropes now over his chest and biceps as well as thighs and calves, binding him tighter than before. He screamed and he yelled and he thrashed within his bonds while one giant of a man grabbed his wrist and turned it over, baring his palm to the room, his fingers closed tight in a fist. A second man joined the first, pulling Kit's fingers open, holding him as still as possible while the whip master exchanged his first implement for a cross shaped brand, red hot from the fire. Kit's eyes widened at the implication, and he yelled and screamed and cursed them all as the bright poker came closer and closer to his skin, burning him just from the heat alone before it touched his flesh in the center of his palm, held until the sizzling stopped while he continued to scream. And it was a scream. He couldn't help it. Perhaps, if Kit had been given time to prepare himself, he might have held his tongue, refrained from making a sound at the pain, but he was a prince. He'd been beaten in the lists during training practice. Beaten on the field of battle and walked away from that. But this was nothing like those times. He had no frame of reference for this agony. And it overcame him.

He revived to the splash of icy water down his body, nearly passed out again when the cold touched his burned palm.

He didn't know how long he'd been unconscious, but he didn't think long given that the man before him was still holding a red brand in his gloved hands.

Kit's other hand was quickly dried from his dousing and pried open.

His eyes widened, unbelieving and yet not shocked they would maim both of his hands so.

"So you don't forget the lesson, little boy."

The poker came down across his skin, as intense and agonizing as the first time.

He panted through it, met his tormentor's stare with a snarl and baring of teeth.

"Good show, old boy, but not enough. Tip him."

The goons turned his chair over, flipping it to its back, letting him fall onto the flagstone floor, his head striking the ground, spots dancing before his eyes at the crash. His hands clenched into fists unthinking. The raw wounds were agony, searing through his brain, shortening his breath. That pain was not enough to distract him from the hands now grabbing his right foot, the heat coming closer to his skin.

He screamed for them.

He screamed at the agony as they burned the bottoms of his feet, no chance of him running if he were set free, no chance of him grabbing for a weapon if one was left within his reach.

They hadn't asked him a question.

Dear gods, ask him a bloody question.

He'd tell them whatever they wanted. Over the river, through the woods, across the stream, back again, he didn't care. Find the camp. Let him go. Stop the burning, please, stop.

He blinked and the world shifted reformed around him from the dark nothing his moment's reprieve of unconsciousness granted. Black stones rose above him into eternity. He couldn't see the top of the dungeon they were holding him in. This was no temporary shelter. This place of pain and evil was something that had stood for a long while. The stones of the building were blackened from years of fires left to burn out and smoke.

He blinked, but his focus frayed all the more until the glow of the fire just beyond him caught his attention, was all he could see, blocked as a shadow passed before it, replaced a dying brand back into the flame. Kit watched the fires churn, smelled the remnants of skin burning away. His skin, from his hands and feet, burning away from the brand whose scar he would forever bear now. He blinked, but his eyes remained closed.

"Throw him in a cell. We'll continue after supper. Venison, yes?"

Don't yield, Prince. Never yield.

He wouldn't. He wouldn't yield. He'd promised; he'd promised his mother; he'd promised Eli. Hadn't he?

The bindings around his body were cut; his arms were pulled above his head and he felt the pain as his right shoulder popped back into place and the wound at the left opened and bled freely once more. He was dragged to a cell, left lying on the cold, unclean floor. He didn't make a sound. The world faded away.

Three

He lost track of time, or stopped counting the days and hours and tortures he endured.

Master Simeon came every day.

Kit liked to think of the man's arrival as morning, his only contemplation on the world beyond the gray black walls of his prison, his hell. The sun didn't touch this dungeon he was relegated to. Night came when Simeon left and the guards opened his cell door and the doors of the few other prisoners within this wretched place, leaving him alone to their tender mercies. He'd screamed himself hoarse the first week. It had taken another before his throat was too swollen to make a sound above a whimper, not that he didn't try. That he could still feel the pain in his body, the beatings, the rapes, the pokers and the whips, broke him. Shouldn't he feel nothing after a time? Shouldn't he become numb?

In point of fact, the torture master was genius, never letting Kit adjust to a particular style before a new implement was added to his torment. Wounds healed, and then were reopened in new ways. His chest was covered in scars, his thighs and arms. Kit didn't want to consider what his back looked like.

The fire was the worst. Before his body was too weak to fight, those first days when he'd still had hopes of surviving this, being rescued quickly, he'd tried to escape. Feet and hands burned, hung from a hook in the ceiling, they'd left him there while they went upstairs for a midday meal.

His shoulder aching from being popped back into place without a chance to heal, the other burning from its wound, he'd managed to wrap the chains around his wrist, pull himself up, hoping to find a rafter high above to hide upon, out of reach of his tormentors. The other prisoners yelled for Simeon. Simeon came running before Kit had managed more than a few feet off the ground. That was the first night the other poor sods given a reprieve from their torture by his presence were allowed into his cell. Honestly, he should have expected the rape. And he had, the master had no boundaries and if it would hurt, then he would use it against Kit.

They'd pissed on him when his body was too broken to perform or use anymore, when their bodies were wrung dry. Cuts and bruises and worse remained when consciousness found him at the end of a bucket of water the next morning. It took three buckets to clean him to Simeon's liking, the second and third salt water to ensure he did not enjoy their ministrations. He grew used to the salt and sting.

Day by day he lost himself to the agony. He found himself laughing when they would chain him in the center of the dungeon for morning washings. Laughing, when the fire was stoked and the red pokers removed to renew the burns on hands and feet, see what raised skin looked like on chest and thigh and groin. Laughing, when the knives and the whips danced before his vision. He cried at the agony of it, screamed and cried like a boy and not a man.

And he laughed.

CR&SO

When was it exactly that he could no longer recall where his camp was?

At some point, all directions, all knowledge of the prince's camp fled his broken mind. He should know. There was something he was supposed to remember and know but for the life of him he couldn't recall it and they kept asking, day after day, and he had no answer to give them so he laughed because laughing made him cry and Master Simeon wanted him broken and he was broke.

Kit...

The memory of her voice would flit through his mind. Her voice. He didn't know who she was anymore. He should probably know who she was, who he was.

Kit.

Yes, that's what Master Simeon called him. That was his name.

Kit.

The master had a bucket of coals spread over the floor. He was lifted on chains, hung above the hot embers.

Master asked where the prince was.

Here, here; I'm here, Kit screamed.

Master said he wanted the truth or he would make Kit burn.

Kit cried as he was lowered to the coals.

Master smiled and let the chains drop and kit could not hold his own weight against his pain and fell to the burning floor.

kit screamed when the fire burned into his already blackened skin.

The kit begged the master please no more.

Master said to answer and he would stop hurting the kit.

The kit screamed at the blisters forming on his flesh.

Master had a bucket of water poured over him, but the coals still burned where they stuck to his skin. Not his face or hair; must not let his hair burn or the brain would burn too.

That's what the Master told his minions who poured more water over the kit to put the fire finally out and he laid in the hissing coals because he could not move, dared not move, hoped no movement would kill him.

The bad men held the kit down in the night.

The coals hurt worse than the bad men.

The bad men said his flesh was warmed by the coals. Bad men were too timid to touch the red embers and bring them to the kit to warm him for their use.

The kit stared at the cell bars. Tears slipped over his cheeks. He stopped trying not to cry.

ଔଞ୍ଚ

The kit could not move from his cell. Bad men, Master's men, dragged him from his prison. Bad men dropped him on the floor. The kit stared at the door bad men left through.

The kit was alone for the first time since the Master came.

Kit…

It hurt to make his fingers move, pull him over the stone floor. The burns made him weak but he was alone and he needed to find the voice in his head. He had to find it now before the voice was gone and the Master returned.

"You have had him for a month and he's told you nothing! What do I pay you for?"

The door opened to the Shouting Man.

Bad men swarmed around Shouting Man, rushed down the stairs and pulled the long knife the kit scrabbled for from him. Bad men beat him. Kicked him and beat him and the kit curled on the ground and could barely see through swollen eyes the dark stone around him.

Shouting Man grabbed the kit's hair. Shouting Man pulled the kit's head back and then dropped the kit to the ground. The kit sobbed. Help me, uncle, the kit tried to say. But the words would not come, and the kit watched his uncle stand back and kick out and there was a snap in the kit's torso and pain speared through him, fresh pain that stole his breath and his whimpers and sobs and the darkness returned.

Uncle shouted and Master bowed and pleaded.

Master smiled red and Master fell in front of the kit. Master's eyes stared into the kit's. Master got to die, but not the kit.

Warm came from Master and flowed over the kit's numb fingers and down the kit's flesh and turned his skin pink in the dark night of the dungeon.

"The new torturer will be here at dawn. If the rat doesn't speak then, kill him. There are enough soldiers trapped in these woods to capture and use who will be of more use. We've only a weak before *Losfidalia Quantir Forseith.* He must die before the gods return. The walls must fall so I might rein."

Bad men agreed.

The kit was left where he lay.

Uncle Shouting Man left through the door and slammed it closed.

Kit shivered on the floor.

Only one more day, and they would let him die.

There was something he was supposed to remember, someone he couldn't remember. He couldn't remember himself. That must be it.

Kit.

Chapter II
One

For a moment, only a moment, she felt him, felt the pain and agony of his soul reaching out for hers. In the Darkness of her dreams, she felt him, a brief brush of his mind against her own, drawing her north, north beyond the woods to a place of stone and darkness and men swarming a room bound round with metal bars.

Eli woke from the vision, bolted from her bedroll in the prince's camp and barely found the slop bucket before her stomach heaved and she fought to get control of herself. She needed to speak to the General. She could find Kit. She could find their prince.

C820

The man was discussing strategy at a table in his tent, sleepless as he'd been for the past month since their prince had vanished, been captured.

"A tower. Where is there a tower dungeon? They're holding him there."

Marius looked at her, his eyes glazed from exhaustion, incomprehension shining in his gaze.

"Kit's there, in a tower dungeon. We need to find him now."

"There are no towers around here, Eli. The closet one is Kravn's Keep. Kravn has been in contact with the king. There has been no sighting of the prince near him. For the gods' sake, Eli. Kravn is Kit's uncle. He's been searching as hard as we have for our prince."

"I am telling you, Marius, General, he is there. Kravn is lying."

"He is the King's brother."

"Fuck the king's brother, and fuck the king. I'm telling you Kit is there."

She knew. She could feel it in her soul. She could feel him, snatches of moments throughout their lives, moments of heartache, of pain, of fear, but always him. Always when he needed her or when she needed a brief moment of knowing he was alive and somewhere in the world with him.

She'd known since the moment he danced with her nearly four hundred years ago. She might have denied the binding between them, done her best to deny it and break it, and ignore it, but it was there, and every day he was missing, a piece of her died knowing he was out there alone and she couldn't find him.

But she knew where he was now.

Her heart was struggling to beat. Her breaths were labored in her chest. Her limbs felt numb and swollen yet physically there was nothing wrong with her. She felt nothing within her flesh to account for her weakness yet she was weak and death was dogging her steps and if she could feel the devil chasing her, he must already be at Kit's side. There was no time left. She knew her prince was standing on the threshold and if he was not saved soon, he would not be saved. Not soon. Soon was too long from now.

"I beg you, Marius. Listen to me. He will die by sunset if we do not rescue him now."

"Out."

The other members of the General's command fled at the anger in Marius' voice.

She watched his careful movements as he placed his palms flat on the table between them, staring down at the map on his desk instead of looking at her.

"You have never trusted me and I—"

"How did you get through the patrols to meet us here?"

She stilled. Her breath, her heart, her mind, stilled at his question. He did not know who she was, who she had been before that night on the road after the ball with the prince. Kit would never have told her secret, but this commander was not an idiot, was not dumb nor ignorant but a force to be reckoned with at all times, on the battlefield and in the strategy tent.

He knew she was of the woods, hadn't questioned that she was an elf, well, had but never let that question dictate to him. He knew she couldn't enter the wood and he could guess why.

But Kit would never have told him who she was, no matter what, the choice was hers.

"Three hundred and some years ago, when you were still earning your place under my command, word reached me that a new Elichi had been chosen for the woodland realm. Rumor said that the previous Priest of the Sword was young, in her prime, not expected to fall for a lifetime or longer and yet less than a hundred years into her rein, she was replaced in her position. Eli. Elichi. It is not a name so much as a title."

"The title means nothing. It is the skill that grants the title that is the prize."

"How did you get through the patrols, Eli? We are ringed round and cornered here. There is no way through or past without meeting the full force of the army sent to cage us, without braving the woods denied you. This was a well-planned attack. This is a coup. The only reason our enemies have yet to take the city is that they believe the prince still alive in our guard and are searching for him. They have not realized their prize is within their grasp and has been for a month or more. But you were not here when the patrols began. You do not hunt these woods or any other and never have. Yet he was captured, and you came on swift wings, but there was no breaking of the ring around us. How did you get through the patrols, Elichi?"

"I am no longer that person. Three hundred years ago the title was stripped from me. I am not that title any longer."

"You were of the forest. Four men died by your hand. The banishment stands for four hundred years and it has not been that many. Yet you are here, and the patrols remain unhindered. How did you find us?"

"The woods were not guarded but by those who name them home."

"You killed four men, four of your own men, to save my prince once before. How many did you kill to come to his aid now?"

"They are not my people any longer."

"How many?" He slammed his fist on the table, and she did not understand this anger he had at her presence.

"Why does it matter?"

"Because I cannot find him, yet here you are saying you can and I do not know that I can trust you with my heart!"

And there it was, the truth she had known for a lifetime or more, and that she did not think her prince realized. She'd given in to that truth, obeyed it, knowing her claim was as valid, more so, than this man's, but she hadn't said that, and Kit had suffered, and was suffering now. She'd spent nearly a hundred years as a shadow so this man could love her prince and her prince could find another because she was nothing to her own people, would never be enough in the view of his.

But the general and she loved the same man. And, by the Darkness that Covers the World, she prayed the prince loved her more than his friend she shared this tent with.

She would give the only answer a man as in love as herself would accept. "Yours is not the only heart that will fail without him."

He met her gaze with tears in his eyes. To see a man so overcome ate at her soul. It was a reason she made a terrible priestess under her mother's rule. She hated the pain of a wounded heart, would rather destroy that sorrow than rebuild it. She was a killer and made no excuse for her life choices, but she loved too, and that was nearly unforgivable. Her life changed the moment she met Kit, yielded to the need to be near him, to know him. She did not regret that choice.

"I ensured no one of the woods died by my hand in coming for you. They won't kill within their borders, not even the prince they want dead more than any other. It's why you've been safe hunting these woods all these years. They don't kill, but they won't stop anyone else from doing the deed within their woods."

"They would kill you."

"Yes. If they caught me, I would be the exception."

"They did not see you."

"Exiled from the forest does not mean I am no longer a child of it. The Darkness protects its own."

He held her stare, unyielding. She clenched her fingers into a fist, determined not to beat the man for his time in answering, time they did not have to waste. "You are certain in what you've seen?"

"I am certain. On my heart: he is in the tower."

The man leaned over the table between them, his hands dark against the vellum of the map spread out before him. "Then we get him out."

Two

She did not know the king's brother. The man had never been introduced to her, and she had never bothered to introduce herself to the nobles of the court who were not her prince's direct compatriots. What did she care of others? That her heart beat only for him, even if she hated the admittance of the sentiment, was all that truly concerned her.

But the man who stood before her, graying hair, and stone gray eyes, so similar to his nephews, would never be mistaken for anything but nobility. She did not need the ring on his finger nor the announcement of his personal guard to tell her who he was. His harsh appraisal, the leering grin he sent her way as he stared at her, meant nothing but another moment she was from her Kit's side. He laughed, and she stood straight and unbowed before him, letting his idiocy give her time to decide the best way in which to kill him. A knife was too quick for someone so foul.

She might love the king, just a little. The king was part of the man she loved, and so she could not hate him entirely. But this man, if man could describe the type of demon he was, was no family to her, and she had no mercy for him, not for what he'd ordered done to his own nephew, even unknowingly. He'd ordered it done to anyone caught for his greed. He was worse than foul.

"A female. Are you mad?" He turned to look at the men standing at her back.

Dressed in the uniforms of mercenaries they'd killed to reach the keep, the general and the prince's guard did not react to the criticism.

"You asked for the best, and we have delivered her into your keeping."

Kravn, that was the name of this evil, sneered at her and her men. "Kill them all. We'll do the job ourselves." He raised a hand to call his servants forward, men oozing from the hall to circle her and her guards.

"A demonstration, perhaps, my lord?" She did not drop the hood from her head, though tilted her face enough that she could meet the man's eyes.

"Blood will make a lady sick."

"I am no lady."

She moved faster than he could follow. If she so desired, she could likely kill all of those in this tower before they knew she was attacking. It might not be quick enough to stop one of them from slitting her prince's throat, from slitting hers at the same time. Better, instead, to wait, and to fight after Kit was safely away.

So she moved and grabbed the guard at the bastard's back, pulling him against her chest and backing towards her men, dragging him with her. Her knife drew a thin line of blood at his throat, and she smiled at the scent of iron wine in the air.

Her victim clutched at her arm pinning him, and she ignored the scrabbling of his fingers against her.

How long had it been since she used the magic inherent to her people to take a life? How long since she had hunted for the evil that sought to hide in the Dark's embrace?

She'd grown complacent within the borders of the city. She'd called shadows, and fought battles, but she'd foresworn her vow to the Master of the Final Midnight. She was the hand that ushered man to the Darkness.

She could love, for she loved Kit. She could heal, and she'd healed for Kit. But a healer's gifts could be turned dark so easily. Pinch a nerve in the arm, and the hand would go numb. Leave the vein closed and the flesh would bloat with blood unable to return to the heart. So easy, to crush bone housed within the thin covering of skin, watch said skin sag without a skeleton to hold it erect.

She leaned in to her victim's throat, her words carrying easily in the room. "If it is any consolation, I will kill you when

I am done with you. But until then, know agony." A thought was all it took for his arm to shatter, bone snapping through skin at her will. No, not enough though, not nearly enough for the thoughts she read in this man's mind, the vision of the broken body in the cell below that had not suffered like this but had suffered worse in so many ways.

"Qui forlcrum domini galrustion."

Know the agony he knows.

She forced the memories of Kit's torture to this man's mind, that which this man had inflicted she returned to him tenfold, and when he screamed himself hoarse, she willed his arm gone, and the flesh unraveled, and blood and bone dissolved beneath her will, exposed only for a moment to the watching eyes of the men around her before the limb was eaten by the Darkness of the night that her kind called God, that her people worshipped as That Which Covered the World and was Inescapable.

Eli let the male drop from her grasp, slitting his throat as he fell forward to writhe on the ground at her feet in his last moments before Death claimed him. The Darkness consumed him, leaving no flesh, no ash, no blood or remembrance of the body that once had been behind. Only the clothing, untouched by her magic and her fury.

For so long she had kept a leash on this side of herself, enjoying her life in Kit's court, a life of blood and death and the battle and dance of swords, but pure, untainted by the magic of her mother's court. She was the Elichi. She was the Daughter of the Darkness, the Priestess of Final Midnight, the only female to earn the title as the ruthless killer who was Justice to those deserving of a harsh end, Mercy to those who begged a quick death.

She hadn't forgotten this side of herself.

Kit hadn't shied from it when they were at war and she fought to save his life and her own. He'd held her when she fought back the madness trying to claim her.

Kit had renamed her.

A title is not a name, he'd said.

It was not a name, no, but it was who she was, and it was so much more than just a nightmare told to scare little city dwellers into sleeping through the night.

She was Eli.

The men at her back grasped at their swords, ready to draw them against her.

She fought back the Darkness, because she wasn't vengeance here, she wasn't justice.

She was the captain of Kit's guard. She was here for the man she loved, the man who was dying in the dungeon below her feet.

Today she was not the Dark's Mistress, and she could not let the demands which once consumed her do the same now.

She fought the darkness, and it was Marius, standing at her back, who placed his hand against her shoulder, gave her a touchstone to cling to. Hers. These men were hers. They would fight for her, and she would fight for them.

She took a breath, sent waves of whispering dreams of happier times to her men, soothing them like their mothers would, rocked to sleep in warm embraces.

The men of the keep, she wrapped in fear so that they would remember who and what she was, and they would give her what she wanted, even if they didn't realize she wasn't there for his death.

"You're from the woods."

Her smile was hollow, pulled at her skin grown too tight to her bones. She was not herself, flooded by the power that was her birthright and her damnation. If she was lost to it now, he would die, her prince would die and she would die with him. Her death did not frighten her as much as losing him did. For a moment, for a breath, she broke apart, lost herself to the power swirling within her veins, to the rage at the injustice it sought to fight. For a moment, she was not herself but who she once was, and then Marius' hand tightened, and her mind was her own again.

The king's uncle bowed to her; bowed to her power and her terror.

"Where is he?"

But she knew the answer. Down the stairs, beyond the door. He waited for her. He did not know she was here, but he was waiting and she'd come.

The traitor pointed at the door behind her, and she turned to face her men standing terrified guard at her back. They were afraid of her. The acrid scent of sweat filled the air, fists gripped swords like they had a chance of stopping her at her zenith. She felt the surge of dark approval in her veins at their terror, and had to fight hard against it.

She could kill them all. It would be easy. A thought, a whisper, a touch as innocuous as a brush of fingers against a closed fist and they would die, screaming in agony, and she could walk free.

But there would be no coming back from the killing edge. There would be no hope for her if she took all these lives, some unclaimed by the Darkness, some worth saving under the Night's Eye.

If she gave in, she would be nothing more than a vessel of the Black, and she did not know if she would remember to spare Kit if she was consumed.

Marius stood strong, stood before her, met her gaze to bring her back to their place amidst the demons in this hellhole. Oh, she could see the terror there. He might have offered his touch to ground her, but it was a weak thing. He was trusting her with his heart, and he didn't know if that trust was misplaced, and until she saw Kit, saved Kit, she didn't know that she could get enough control of herself not to be a threat to the men she had adopted as her family. She knew there was madness in her gaze, but Marius held her stare, and nodded, leaving the way free to her approach, her descent.

She blinked her eyes, let the tear fall and knew he watched that last vestige of humanity she claimed as her own dry on her skin before she opened the door and descended into the madness she would either raise her heart from, or die within.

No one stopped her from closing the door at her back.

The fire in the grate was banked. Its heat barely enough to suffuse the small fireplace, let alone the room beyond. Cell doors lined one side of the space. All but one was empty, the men within standing at the bars, staring as she descended into their domain. She kept her gaze on them, stalking from the stairs to stand before their cages and gauging the hearts of the men within.

"All shall die." Her voice held the Dark power still riding her hard. It took a single touch of her hand against theirs before they fell to their separate floors and writhed there. "Tenfold times tenfold. You could have been free, but you stayed to torture him because it was not you who suffered. Tenfold times tenfold. The price is weak for what you have done."

But she didn't have time to exact greater retribution than that.

Not vengeance.

Vengeance was for the weak; those who needed to clean their souls by the shredding of their persecutors.

No, this was Retribution.

Payment in kind.

A thought froze their vocal chords, silenced their screams so they were denied even that small outlet of escape from their suffering.

Her gaze fell on the one she'd come for, and she would not be distracted from him any longer.

Carefully, for he flinched at the slightest sound, she made her way to the center of the chamber and her prince lying naked there. He did not shiver nor look to her. There was not a place unmarked on his body, bruises and bleeding covered him, blackened his eyes and burned his arms and chest.

"Kit."

She knelt at his side, but he made no sound but to drag in a breath that rasped and barely supplied him with air. The cloak she wore was warm, meant to cover him while they subdued the keep and brought him to safety. Her cloak was meant to give him comfort, but if she covered him with the heavy cotton lined with fur, the weight would bury him. Skin and bones. Gone was the graceful prince she'd known, the soldier, the warrior, the dancer, her comfort. Left was only a corpse kept breathing by a will likely broken to basic thought, too afraid to die and yet begging for the sweet release all the same.

A sob tore from her throat, her hands hesitating over his skin, afraid even to brush aside the cinders clinging to burns layering his flesh. "Kit."

He eyes fluttered, barely able to open beneath the bruising that swelled them closed.

His lips parted but no sound emerged.

Still, she read the words he spoke in silence.

"I know you."

"Yes. I'm here. I'm here, Kit. I'm here."

His hand rose from the ground, not far, barely enough to notice, but it rose and she reached for him, lifting his swollen fingers, his burned palm, to her cheek, burying the fury at his torture deep inside so that he would not feel the cold wash of her rage, would not flinch away from her.

"Ella." His fingers curled against her cheek, brushing her skin with his knuckles. He smiled at her, a brief upturn of lips cracked and bleeding. "Love—"

If she hadn't been holding his hand, it would have fallen to the cold stone floor the moment the last of his breath left his lungs. She pulled him closer, felt the stopping of her own heart as he died before her and she was powerless to save him.

No, not powerless, not yet.

She channeled the despair in her spirit, the Dark power of destruction that her mother used as the greatest healer of the Dienobolos.

She was her father's daughter, she knew that, but she'd done her mother's will from time to time. She could heal him.

Please gods, Merciful Darkness, just once, she needed her strength and her magic to respond to her will as it was meant to, as she desired because she could not lose him, not yet, not now, not when she had only just found him, when there was too much left unsaid between them, too much left undone. She held his hand to her heart and pressed her hand to his, formed the circle between dead and living and breathed into it, willing her life to be his, their souls to finish the binding between them.

The world shuddered.

Not the dungeon, not the ground at her feet, but the world in total, that which was her home and beyond the woods she'd grown up in. The world shuddered, and died, expelled a breath that was held deep within the bowels of the earth and shattered. Or would have shattered, for her breath filled his lungs, and his heart beat a painful staccato within his chest and the world steadied, reformed to his life beat, held together for a moment more.

Sweet Night.

It was not the walls that would fall if he died. Not just the walls within which he lived and was meant to rule. Why had his gods made him the fate of the world? How could no one have ever guessed at that truth? He was far more precious and far more important than any had known, and she did not have the skill to hold him to this life for very long.

A thought opened the door to the dungeon, brought Marius to the stone steps to look down upon the hell his prince was forced to live in.

She could hear the fighting, the battle waged above.

Marius would have guarded the door for her retreat, for his prince's retreat.

Brave man, to stand and face her after her demonstration above. Likely no other had been willing to take the post.

"We need a healer. He won't last much longer and I cannot carry him from here alone."

The commander nodded, rushing from the doorway to her side, Kit's side. The man did not know where to lift, no place free of pain on Kit's body, their movements bound to cause more agony than spare any. Still, they managed to raise their prince, his arms slung about their shoulders.

Eli looked to the stairs, expecting their enemy to walk through the door and block their path. But it was not their enemy she saw, and the guards who defended their retreat nodded to her, fear in their gazes, yes, but respect too.

They managed to get Kit up the stairs.

At the top, the commander passed Kit to another soldier, taking post to get them from the building.

She knew the moment Kit returned to consciousness, the moment he tensed against her hold on him, prepared himself for whatever new torment awaited him. "We're getting you out of here, love. Stay with us now, we're getting you out of here."

"ELF!"

She turned at the call, looking at the stairway leading to the upper levels of the keep and the raging bastard whose sword even then pierced the belly of one of her men, her ally, her friend. She turned to the call, and Kit turned with her.

She did not expect him to know who the man was. That Kit was aware enough to tense, for a rage as dark as her own to pour out from his spirit, was a terrifying thought, not that it was undeserved, but that she was infecting him with her own Darkness. In the moment it took her to think the thought, he lurched from her grip, overbalanced and she had to scramble to keep him from tumbling to the floor. He hung limp from her side, choking on blood that welled past his lips, the purple around his ribs enough to know that the broken bones had finally caught an organ and pierced through. She should have been more careful, known better than to stop and turn. He coughed, and smiled, and she looked to see Kravn fall from his perch on the stairs, tumble over the banister and land on the ground of the main floor, the knife Kit'd thrown piercing the man's heart.

The fighting stopped for a moment; the mercenaries' leader dead on the floor.

Eli thought that perhaps they would disperse, they would be free to leave with the master dead.

A cry split the castle, and the fighters yelled to augment the bellow, renewing their attack for the spirit of their dead leader.

"We need to get out of here."

Marius must have heard her over the din, sword slicing into the torso of his opponent, clearing a space for them to escape into, rush the main doors and into the waiting dawn of the day beyond.

She helped her partner lift Kit into the cart they'd brought with them, climbed in after her prince and shifted until she could rest his head in her lap, keep him within her arms while they fled.

Her soldiers filed out, the men rushing from the keep, Marius the last to leave, supervising the retreat.

She must have known, deep in her soul, that one of them would not leave this place alive. He must have known that the better option would be to save her life at the cost of his own.

He stood in the castle doorway, his men mounting their horses, preparing to flee, the remainder of their guard already ranged in the forest as escort for them all. Marius stood in the doorway, and turned back to the keep, closing the portal behind him, remaining to stall whatever men still lived so they had a chance to escape.

"NO!"

But her word was mistaken, and the driver of the cart snapped the reins and the horses flew forward, into the woods, away from this terror, towards a hoped for safety.

There were mercenaries in the woods, still blocking their path.

They needed a healer or he would not make the journey from this place.

His breathing stuttered, his eyes opened wide with his panicked, strangled breath. She pressed her hand to his sternum, felt the Black of her magic rush down her arms in flowing vines, weave from her flesh to his and bolster what little strength remained within him.

"Get us to the woods!"

"They'll kill us, my lady."

"I'm your fucking captain! Get us to the godsdamned woods and I will get us past their patrols. We need the Priestosolos. She's the only hope he has."

"The elves will kill us same as the mercs!"

"Leave them to me."

She matched her breathing to his, forced her spirit into his flesh, his body to yield to her will. She held him to his flesh, refused to let him die though death must have been a relief to all that he had suffered. She kept him alive, and spread before her a plea for sanctuary, a call for aid, her magic spiraling into the roots below the wheels of the cart, the branches reaching far into the woods, the forest answering her plea as they barreled deeper into the trees.

Called by a priestess of the wood. Begged by a priestess of the wood. Summoned by a priestess of the wood.

Her once people met them at the boundary of glade and forest, rode herd on her guards and spirited them along the hidden paths to the center of the Priestosolos' territory and the greatest healer in this realm. She kept her hand to his heart, let her tears fall unheeded down her cheeks as the beating beneath her palm stuttered and pleaded to stop.

They raced through the woods, and she knew her once brethren gathered close not for his protection, but to ensure that she did not escape what justice was owed. They raced to salvation and doom.

Merciful Night, let them see his life is what keeps ours from dying. Do not let him die. Do not let us die.

Three

The elves swarmed them when the cart came to a stop in the center of the wood. Eoa, the Mother Tree, as large around as a house and taller than ten stories, rose in the center of the grove, the beacon of the Dienobolos and their worship. From the trees surrounding the mother wood, Eli's people stood with bows pointed to the ground, safe within their flying homes, guarded by the branches and leaves the rooms were built into.

No one moved, not her brethren, nor the guards.

"Isto fortuis rad'lichoi eist."

Her mother walked from the hewn doors of the great tree, the oak having been hollowed out over the centuries to form the Temple to the Darkness all elves worshiped. The High Priestess would not forgive Eli's betrayal. Already she called all arrows to be turned upon Eli in the cart. The Dienobolos would not miss when they let the bolts fly. Eli would die with the shaft of an arrow through her heart if her mother were merciful. But her mother had called for imprisonment first, and it would not be a quick death she faced.

By the breaking of her exile, returning to the wood, Eli accepted the death sentence she'd earned herself. She'd called for sanctuary though, and once invoked, in the Darkness' name, her mother and her brethren were bound to offer respite until words were broken amongst the elves and those seeking refuge.

"She has invoked Sanctuary, Priestosolos."

Eli did not know the man who walked boldly towards her mother. Once, upon a time, Eli had been so bold too.

Priesto, a Priest of the Dark. *Solos*, the highest amongst men.

From the moment of her birth, Eli knew her mother only as the High Priestess. The woman who bore her showed the same love and devotion to all her people, blood bound or not. When Eli achieved the rank of Elichisolos, it was her mother who made the offering to the Darkness, bound Eli to the Wood and summoned the Night to fill Eli with Its power. That Eli chose to offer death, a warrior and not priest or healer, to the Night, deepened the rift between them, but it was still the only day she remembered feeling her mother's pride in her, and she'd betrayed that by saving this prince. Twice over now.

Her mother was not just priestess, though it was the greatest of her titles.

It was not the priestess that Eli sought to invoke within these woods.

"Lieasolos, I invoke Sanctuary for these men and their prince. I beg the Darkness for Healing as we have too long misunderstood the—"

She would have finished her tale, told her mother that it was not the walls that would fall if Kit died but all the world. She would have spoken the words and offered her truth as proof of them, but her heart lurched within her chest, a painful contraction that staggered her, bent her over her prince as his breath expelled and once more the ground began to shake.

Had she the strength to look about her in that moment, she would have noted the trees quaking to their roots, branches tumbling to the ground without wind or rain to cause the fall. Eoa screamed, a harsh sound of twisting wood and burning forest though no fire swept through the grove.

No, Eli did not look about her and see the destruction of his death. What Darkness was granted to her, what little skill her mother had imparted in healing, Eli poured into his ravaged flesh, held the wisp of spirit not yet flown from his body to this world, used it to reel in the soul of the man she loved, even knowing how desperately pained and willing to die he was.

Her heart beat.

Air filled his lungs.

The tremors of the earth stilled, and she wept for her strength was spent, the Darkness that was her birthright and earned by strength of arms, was light within her, leaving her empty. She could not hold him if he fled his body again. If she could not hold him to her, then she would follow, and be glad for the obliging.

She trembled at his side, not having realized she'd fallen in his plight, unable to even hold him with the weakness in her flesh.

"Please, Lieasolos," her words slurred against her tongue, eyes trying to focus on her mother now in the cart beside her, ancient hands placed to the prince's chest in what Eli feared was a ministration of death. "It is not the walls that will fall."

Four

Eli woke in the clutch of a nest, her body cocooned within the warm embrace of branches piled high with blankets and hot stones. The gentle hand caressing her forehead soothed her, calmed her, tempted her to burrow back into the warm embrace of slumber and forget the world around her.

Her eyes opened wide, staring at the woman sitting at her side, the woman staring back.

"Did you know, when you spared him all those years ago, the truth of his life?" Her mother spoke in their native tongue, a language Eli expected to hear only curses in before she died, yet this was a simple question asked with an unassuming tone.

"No, Priestosolos."

The priestess' fingers moved to Eli's throat, testing the strong pulse beating there though the ache remained deep in Eli's chest, not all from Death waiting too close to claim her, *him*.

"Did you bond him, knowing we would not kill you once we learned his death would kill the world?"

She had not meant to bond him at all. Knowing her death would mean his in the end offered no comfort to her. She'd felt his suffering when she'd taken stupid risks over the years, faced Death and survived to tell the tale and he'd waited for her return, never knowing how close his end came at her hands. Had she known what bonding to him would mean, had she known that she'd committed the act without thought or knowledge of how it was done, she would have reversed it post haste. Was it too late to do so now? If anyone knew how it was undone, it would be the High Priestess; and if Eli begged mercy from the Dark, the Night might answer kindly and allow her life to be severed without the loss of his. "I offer my life in payment for the ones I've taken. I beg only that you separate the bond you speak of. Let him live, Priestosolos, I beg it of you and the Darkness that Claims us all."

"You did not answer my question, child."

"I bound to him the night the brethren attacked, Priestosolos."

"And when did you learn that his death heralded the death of us all?"

"When he died in my arms in the dungeon they held him in." The anger and bitterness and self-hatred were clear in her voice. The man she loved, the man she had given everything up for, had only grown more and more enamored of over the years, had died, not once, but twice in her arms and she was too late to save him. No, that was not precisely true. She hated herself because he should never have known such suffering.

Tears slipped from the corners of her eyes.

She swiped at them, closing herself to emotion as befit the position she once held within the Dienobolos. She would not shame herself or them by crying over fate's fickle ways.

"Can you sever the bond between us? Can you spare him from the taking of my life? Whatever I must do, I offer it to you in payment, but I beg you," how desperately she wanted to plead to her mother but spoke only to the priest instead, "I beg you, do not make him suffer further."

The Priestosolos stared at Eli, a gentle hand making idle circles on Eli's chest as she laid on her back in her bower. The hand stilled over her heart, the longest finger tapping out the rhythm that coursed blood through Eli's body, life into her. "There is a way to do what you ask, to sever the claim your heart has laid on him. This I could do for you."

Eli looked away from her mother, stared into the limbs of branches above her head that created a second floor. Many times as a child she'd run through the massive tree, trailing her fingers over the burrowed nests within its thick trunk. She sang to the injured or the ill that remained within the wooden nests as they were treated by her mother, the healers within the order of *Liaea*.

So many aspects of the darkness: the priests who prayed to the night, to *Pirie* in the Darkness; the healers worshipping the *Liaea*, the inner blackness of the body never to touch the sun. *Echi*, Master of the Final Midnight, the End of All Things, harbinger, guardian. *Rouchim*, the gatherer, the nurturer, Lady of the Earth, Keeper of Secrets; *Ashet*, the laborer, the sentinel, Lord of the Forge, Harnesser of the Light. All aspects of the One Darkness, all housed here, within Eoa, the temple that stretched into the Eve.

She could have offered herself to the *Liaea*, used the darkness to heal, or help or forge or honor, but she'd chosen *Echi*, been the Master's Darkness come to Man, and now that darkness betrayed the life she wished most to save.

She heard the 'but,' in her mother's voice. Her death would not be so simple as the breaking of a bond. Though exiled from the wood, she'd been a daughter of it still, worshipping the stars in the heavens that illuminated the Night, gave It shape and soul. Priestosolos could break the bond between Kit and Eli, but Eli would lose the Night as her guardian in the sundering.

"No, Daughter."

Eli blinked away the moisture in her eyes, turning her head once more to the woman at her side.

"You are, and will always be, a child of the Night. Your soul was anointed by the Darkness and that can never be turned away. I can break your bond to the boy—"

"Prince. He is no boy, has not been for many years."

Her mother nodded. "—the prince. It would be a simple thing to turn your heart from the beating of his. But I cannot turn his heart from yours, Iisforsos."

Iisforsos.

First to Walk Among the Stars.

Eli's brow furrowed. "I do not understand."

"Let us see to your prince, and then I will explain."

"Priest—"

"Come, Daughter, we've spent enough time here. Your prince is beginning to spiral again."

She'd forgotten that the *Lieasolos*, once ascribed to a healing, was bound into the being she worked with. Her mother would know every tortured breath Kit took, each stuttered beat of his heart. Eli tried to ignore her own bonding to the man. It was hard enough to imagine giving him up, but she would make the sacrifice gladly, even if, as her mother said, his heart was bound to hers. Rather he should live and she die. His life was all she wanted for him.

Eli struggled to free herself from the tangle of blankets surrounding her. The nest was warm, but it did not help the chill chasing down her spine. She missed having him at her back, knowing he was there when she slept, or would come at the rise of the night. She missed his hand extended to help her rise when dawn chased the black from the sky.

The hand she took now was cold in comparison, old where his was once young and supple. Would his hands be the same ever again? She knew the burns that covered his flesh.

She missed the smile when he met her gaze in the morning, missed the returning of it on her own lips.

"Come."

Eli walked at the high priestess' side down the winding path that climbed the inner walls of the tree trunk. The bed she'd been given was on the fifth spiral so the descent took time, though the silence between them was calm and peaceful.

Still, her heart beat faster the nearer they drew to the main floor. She dared not look over the railing as she would have to step to her mother's right hand to do so. She did not deserve to walk in such a place. But the closer they drew to the temple proper, the greater the pull of his misery became.

"You put him on the altar?"

His blood would waken the Darkness. He was not a disciple of the woods. He could not make the same offering, suffer the same acceptance as she or her mother or any other of the Dienobolos made.

Eli made to push past the high priestess, very nearly succeeding in getting around her mother and to the aisle leading to the dais before the breath was stolen from her lungs and she dropped to the floor, choking as she tried to breathe but no oxygen came to her.

The Priest passed her, and air returned.

Eli gasped in great lungfuls, coughing though all she wanted was to sprint to Kit's side, protect him from whatever the Priestosolos would do. She managed a strangled "Please," but her mother did not turn back to her, continued down the path into the darkened Sanctuary and the secrets held within.

She fought to her feet.

Eli pulled herself along the rows of pews, sobbing at the blackness beyond the portal. It would not matter if they saw her tears. She would die in this place either with his last breath or when her life was taken for returning before her exile was complete. Let them see why she chose the man on the slab over them; let her heart make their hatred wane or grow, she didn't care.

The few who lingered within the pews made no move to help or hinder her. They did not turn their heads to her sobs, stumbling along after the High Priestess to the sanctuary and the Dark beyond.

Eli lurched through the doorway. Her hands broke her fall on the hard wood flooring, scraped and bled into the grain.

Only once before had she been in this room. Her eyes had been bound, her wrists tied above her head. Five strikes of the whip, one for each aspect of the Night. But she came as a supplicant of the Echi, and suffered five more for the Master's pleasure. Through the wounds, the Darkness found her; her blood drawn and offered to the Black. She walked from the temple bloodied but alive. It took her fourteen days to see through the void and for light to pierce her eyes, make her more than the wrathless Judgment of the Echi, give her back part of the humanity her offering to the Dark obscured.

She had not seen the interior of this sanctum then.

She did not look now, her attention focused on the robed men and women around the body lying so still on the stone center of the temple.

"Elichi—" The priest, healer, who spoke turned the attention of the others Eli's way.

She was weak. She could not fight with the strength and speed with which she was accustomed. That did not stop her from attacking the three who made towards her. Triplets in robe and power. The Darkness did not call for the sacrifice of their lives.

Eli screamed, flipped one of the elves over her shoulder, another she felled with a short jab to his groin.

Kit thrashed on the slab, seizing while she fought and her mother joined with the other priests to surround him, those battling Eli subduing her only as her breath floundered once more, this time do to the man dying atop the table, and not the magic of the Priest.

"NO!"

A wave of magic pulsed from her, moving those gathered around her love away, keeping their hands which could do so much damage from his flesh. She would not let them hurt him. She had begged for sanctuary.

Her legs collapsed beneath her. The three ignored the hand she raised in warding against them. They knew as she did that she did not have the strength to attack again. She crumbled to the wood, her forehead touching the smooth grains, begging, but she did not know if it was to the Dark or to priests she plead.

The healers came no further and she managed to lift her head enough to watch them flood back to the slab and press their hands against Kit's flesh as they had been before she came before them.

"Elichi," this time her name broke through her emotions, settled her in the room with the healers working to stabilize a body broken beyond what it could endure. "Help us save him."

The Priestosolos held Eli's gaze, the Darkness eclipsing the white of her eyes as she bent her will to saving the prince.

Save him.

Yes, she could save him, Eli would save him.

But she did not know how. She knew how to grant Mercy, send them into the Darkness. She did not know how to bring them out.

Her mother's power encompassed her, soothed her. Frayed nerves were sewn together, helping her find her center, react with more than just emotion.

She rose on unsteady legs, clutching at her chest though the pain was nearly gone.

"Here, Elichi."

Eli was directed to the head of the altar, urged onto its cold stone top. The robed priests gently lifted Kit's head from the slab, her crossed legs a cradle to rest him in. She could not stop herself from stroking over his face, brushing back the matted strands of hair from his forehead. What energy she had went into soothing him, the tears that fell from her eyes onto his face were inconsequential and she brushed them against his skin, the boiling force of magic within her held in each small drop, eased into his body with her touch.

She knew the moment the next seizure came, felt the tensing in his muscles as though they were her own.

Her mother was silent.

Eli didn't know what to do.

The Darkness that had so long been her shadow, her accomplice each time she took up a sword or brought an assailant to their knees, rose up in her, overwhelmed her, reached to destroy and she wrangled the power into a loving caress, stroked into his brow, his arms, his chest, all that she could reach of him, ending the spasms before they began. His breath came no easier, his ribs still broken, his burns still weeping, but he did not thrash, and she prayed that that was enough, that keeping him calm would allow those with her to work their will on the body before her.

She immersed herself in the Darkness.

Her eyes grew blind but for the glow of stars. She could no longer feel him where he laid against her. If she had a body, she did not know it, and it did not matter as she channeled the Night to the seeking hands reaching for her, her soul a conduit as she opened herself to Infinity and lost herself to the Eve.

Five

She floated there, in the nexus of power and energy that surrounded her like a womb, reformed her, sheltered her. There was a reason she was not meant to remain in its warmth. Something, no, someone needed her to return, but the Night was so dark, and the Darkness so complete, that there was nothing to follow to reach that questing something calling her.

She did not want to leave regardless.

The pull was not so great here in the void. She could ignore its tickling presence in the back of her mind if she so chose to do so.

But the Dark began to lighten, the cocoon she had woven about herself to dissolve beneath the fingers peeling apart the wispy layers of the night. No matter how hard she tried, she could not repair the damage, could not stop the spread of sunshine into her bower. It burned her, where it touched, and she scrambled back from its bright embrace, desperately trying to hide, not wanting to return to the OverWorld, enjoying the safety of the Eternity she rested in.

The nagging tug in the back of her mind grew stronger, pulled harder. Her fingers dug into the nest around her and passed through the thick branches like they were a mirage and she was waking from the dream. She cried as she was pulled away, but away she went, and her tears were not enough to hold her to the Night. Warmth covered her cheeks, patted gently, and she opened her eyes to the blinding light she had thought to escape in the Dark. There was too much, and she could not see, but the Dark did not come to rescue her, and she was held tight in solid arms, a heart beating against her ear. She was a daughter of the End, and yet the new day claimed her and she could not get loose.

"Thank the Darkness."

She blinked, and the world focused around her, the last of the Night fading from her eyes. Torches were burning, flicking in and out of her sight as people moved, a great many people, more than there had been, than she remembered when, where, what had happened? Why was she here? Where had she gone?

Her throat was dry, lips parched. "Moth … Priestosolos?"

The older elf smiled down at her, and she could not remember why it was odd for the woman to be doing so. A hand stroked again over her cheek, brushed back knotted strands of hair from her forehead. The woman sang, whispered, hummed softly. There was a reason to fear this woman, but she did not know what it was or why. "Welcome home, Iisforsos."

Was that her name? She could not recall. But the woman, Mother, looked at her with love, with compassion. She must know.

"Calm, Daughter. Hush now. Rest."

There was someone she was supposed to find, something she was supposed to do, to save.

"Rest, Iisforsos. Rest." The command echoed around her, the dark power of her Mother's magic soothed her thoughts, blanketed everything but for the need to sleep, to let go.

Her eyes closed.

Whatever Iisforsos wanted, needed, she would worry about in the morning. It meant nothing within the warm embrace of the arms around her.

Chapter III
One

S ome nights he woke in a cold sweat, unable to recall what visions had danced through his head while he slept. Some nights he didn't wake, and those were worse, having to relive a hell his waking thoughts couldn't remember but for the phantom pains in his body, lingering even after the sun rose. And they weren't all phantom pains. Most still remained with him, aching, unhealed, healing but not quite whole yet. His ribs were the worst, they made sitting in bed an agony, rising and walking and breathing nearly impossible. But remaining abed did little to aid him in feeling whole, feeling competent.

His hands clenched, the skin tight, the muscles aching. Scars covered his palms, marks from a branding iron he remembered in his subconscious, remembered the pain of, but couldn't think back upon. Even staring at the scars made his stomach clench. He started most days hunched over a bowl, his supper, or lunch, whatever food he'd managed to choke down the day before revisiting him. That he was sick made him angry. That he couldn't keep down a meal, that he couldn't stand the thought of being touched or seen, after nearly twelve months, made him nauseous and the process started all over again. He laughed, because he refused to cry any longer. He had no tears left regardless. He didn't remember if he'd cried during his torture. It seemed like a good enough bet that he had. He thought he remembered laughing, for the sound now had a hint of the madness he had grown used to some time ago.

The first time he woke, the first time he stirred from the coma his body slept in, there had been no one with him to calm his shaking, the horrors of his dreams. So weak, he'd barely managed to reach the chamber pot in time for the bile in his belly to spew out. He hadn't been able to get back in his bed. That he knew it was his bed astounded him. He'd cried then, at being home, not knowing how he returned, that no one was there with him. But death shouldn't hurt this badly, so he knew he was still alive, and that was worse.

He refused a manservant, not wanting anyone to witness the sweat that coated his body, nor the scars that he would always bear. The ones on his soul, invisible to the world, were the worst. Every look he received, whether knowing or not of what he'd suffered, he shied from, felt the pity for his survival in their gazes.

A coward would end it. Or was it cowardly to seek such an out in oblivion?

He could do it. If he killed himself, the walls would still stand. The prophecy had come and passed. His life meant nothing to the survival of the city now. The walls were their own again, his death would not crumble them. Five hundred and seventeen, nearly eighteen.

Survive the trials of the year.

No one else had attacked to take his life since his return from Kravn's Keep, from the Dienobo. There could be nothing worse than what he'd suffered already.

Two more months and the year would be over.

If nothing else, he could wait the two more months before he killed himself, just to be safe.

He did not want to wait, and that was the problem.

Perhaps the prophecy wasn't fulfilled then.

The niggling doubt that his life was still the fate of the world was what kept the knife hidden beneath his pillow, sheathed instead of bloodied.

☙❧

"Boy, are you paying attention? The minister asked what you thought of the plans?"

Plans? What plans?

Kit had been sitting in meeting after meeting, hands gripping the armrests of his chair to keep him upright, focusing on every breath he took as pain swamped him. Was it too much to ask to be allowed to curl into a ball and rest for a little while? Not that he ever really rested, but he wanted one night spent without the memories battering his subconscious mind. Almost it would be better to face them head on, but if they were this bad in his sleep, he did not want to know what they would be like awake.

"Apologies, Father, Lord Minister, I fear I am not myself at the moment. If you would leave the plans with—"

He didn't know if he had a secretary. Marius had always been his right hand, despite his position as a soldier and not politician. Kit didn't really know all that many of the nobles, and those he did were little more than passing acquaintances, met from balls he despised or court sessions where they were too busy arguing politics to whisper more than the less than jovial greetings they meted out. Kit didn't even know if it would be appropriate to request one of those simpering fools as his impromptu man of letters.

"Of course, your highness," Minister Grouel smiled. The expression was the same one Kit had received from his tutors when he was still in nappies, condescension masked with required fondness for the heir of an empire. "I'll have everything sent to your rooms for your perusal. We are in no rush."

Which meant that if Kit didn't get through the paperwork by tomorrow night at the latest, all hell would break loose and it would be on Kit's shoulders. Just another thing to weigh on his soul.

"Son, are you alright?"

The king leaned over his throne, his hand reaching towards Kit's clutching at the armrests.

He'd thought the wheezing he heard was simply a bird caught behind the great chairs, or a servant in need of a glass of water. That the sound was coming from him hadn't crossed his mind, and yet, the attention now drawn to it, Kit found himself struggling to draw in a breath, beads of sweat dotting his forehead as he fought not to crumple in his chair. To be proven so weak before ministers and nobles and his father... The thought did nothing to relieve the burgeoning panic in Kit's breast.

He heard someone calling for a physician, a healer, guards to help him back to his chambers. Hands wrapped around his arms, lifting him from the chair and pulling him through the halls of the palace. He knew he was being carried, but his mind focused only on his chest, the feel of a whip breaking skin, a boot to his side and the sickening crunch of connection with his flesh.

Panic attacks had never plagued him.

Yes, after the war he'd been lost in his own head for a time, but not like this, not thrown back into the misery so completely, so unable to separate the past from reality as he was now.

Kit pulled from his guards' arms when they reached his room, stumbling away from them and to the open balcony doors, begging for air, sweet, fresh air, far away from the plague of flagstone walls and a black ceiling that stretched into an eternity he couldn't escape.

No one followed him onto the small ledge. No one spoke to him, or if they did, he did not hear them.

He closed his eyes, soaking in the sun on his face, the warmth and the smell of nature even if he was still in a building too far removed from the glorious earth and the freedom of the tree shadowed paths.

His shoulders bowed over the railing, back bent, relieving some of the pressure on his chest. He shuddered with the hidden memories that were beginning to spill over into his daytime. If they continued, his father would find him unfit to rule.

Gods, but wouldn't that be perfect.

He snorted at the thought.

A lifetime spent learning how to run a country only to be barred from the job because by learning how to rule the country, he'd been placed on the wanted list of everyone else in the world.

And yet, being denied the kingdom, being forced to abdicate before he even took the thrown might well be what he wanted most. To live, freely, without complications, without the responsibility of a hundred thousand people depending on him for safety and security. He could work in the foundry. He'd done it once. Hard labor, yes, but he'd been good at it; the work had made him feel like he'd accomplished something at the end of the day. Worse case, he could sell his sword arm. So the idea of actually battling set his stomach to twisting, but he could do it, if he needed to. He'd spent nearly two hundred years embroiled in blood. No one would question a soldier's scars. He could kill again. He could get away from the palace and the walls and the destiny that had had him kidnapped and tortured, that had called for his death and he'd been too cowardly simply give in to and die. If he'd just told the master...

Master...

The kit...

His knees buckled and he fell to the stone of his balcony, one hand clenched round his middle while the other supported him as his stomach purged of the fig he'd eaten for lunch. He'd gotten good at moving food around on his plate to appear as though he finished a meal though nothing stayed down.

He should be happy he survived.

He would have been happy, but his life had come at the price of hers. He could live with the insanity if she was at his side. Fool woman had taken him to the Woods. Fool woman, she should have gotten herself out and left him to die for Fate's sake.

He wanted Marius to stand next to him on the balcony, his calm presence a balm to Kit's rioting emotions.

He wanted Eli at his left, her hand in his, the quiet acceptance she'd excelled at. She'd laugh at his thoughts, at his planned escape, telling him he was a fool for the consideration. But she wasn't here. And Marius wasn't here.

He was alone, a prince to a kingdom who pitied him and he couldn't fault their opinion as he pitied himself just as much.

He couldn't meet his father's gaze for fear of seeing the same emotion reflected back at him, worse: shame. But it wasn't his father's shame he feared most, not when he looked in a mirror and could not escape the same in his own eyes.

He pushed himself to his feet, turned away from the sky and trees outside, retreated to the hard mattress that was his prison and salvation both. Easier to dream about his horrors than live knowing everyone else imagined their own version for him.

His chest hurt.

His limbs were weak.

He laid down in the bed, and closed his eyes.

He hadn't told the master who he was, what the bastard wanted to know. No, that wasn't true. The master hadn't believe him. He lived because the man was a fool, and Kit was pathetic.

"There will be a ball for your birthday next month. We will celebrate your life, Christophe, your strength in surviving what you have, the fulfillment of the prophecy, the salvation of our City."

"I will not be in attendance."

No one said anything about the rasp in his voice that wouldn't heal. He'd healed as much as he was able now. The healers came every week. Reported to the king that his body was nearly whole. His ribs no longer ached, burnt muscles had miraculously regrown and he'd lost no range of motion despite the damage he'd suffered. The men whispered, when they thought he wasn't listening, that the woodland physicians were miracle workers. They'd healed him, their enemy.

Kit hated the elves with the same passion he hated the memory of his uncle, the loss of Marius, the men who even now rotted in the king's dungeon, held prisoner after attacking the capital trying to find Kit, never knowing he'd fled unwillingly to the forest and beyond their reach. Of course, Kit hadn't heard of their capture until his father's vengeance had been wreaked upon the men. Funny, but he had no pity for the bastards, even if they'd never shown a moment's torment to him.

"You will most certainly be in attendance, Kit. You must show the people that you are whole, that you are my heir and you have overcome what was done to you. It will be the greatest celebration we've ever had for you. It will put all other balls to shame."

"I have hated this tradition since the day I turned thirty and women began throwing themselves at me to catch a prince. These balls have never been about celebrating me."

"This one will be—"

"Father," Kit met the king's gaze, forcing himself not to flinch away from the desperation in the man's eyes. "Have I not suffered enough? I beg you, do not do this to me."

"Tradition—"

"Please, Father."

The old man stared at Kit, and Kit did not shirk away from the hard gaze.

The first ninety-nine balls had been unbearable. She'd been there the hundredth and for the following three hundred plus excruciating experiences. Even when she was silent, ignoring him, knowing she was near, somewhere near, had made getting through the three days manageable. And the past seventeen years when they had fled to each other in the Dark of the night between dances had been magical. This last year, the ring—

Simeon had taken the chain from Kit's throat. He'd taken the ring and thrown it in the fire, the ring Kit wore until he could deliver it to his elf, his captain.

It was the only time Kit had willingly braved the flames.

There was a circle branded into the palm of his right hand, stark against the cross that discolored the rest of his skin.

The master had still taken the ring from him. Kit hadn't asked if it had been found in the ruins of the tower after his father's men destroyed the place upon Kit's survival. No one would have known to look for it anyways.

He looked in his lap, unable to hold his father's gaze any longer, staring at his clenched hands instead.

She wouldn't be his salvation at this ball.

He had no one to turn to.

Surely his father could understand that he could not be around that many people. He no longer had the constitution for it.

"I cannot cancel the ball now, boy. The announcement has already spread. The Arqueanmen have already replied that they will be in attendance, their princess with them. Quiofol has similarly pledged to come. Even the Dienobolos have promised to send representatives to augment our new peace treaty with them."

Yes, a peace treaty that Kit wanted to shred, not caring that he lived by their grace when they'd killed the only woman he ever loved.

Dear gods.

Dear gods, letting the thought invade him reignited every pain he'd suffered, not yet even one year old. And she was the worse pain of all.

"I cannot do this."

"Kit—"

No, he did not want to hear his father's pleas.

He fled the throne room, their court sessions over for the day. He no longer needed to be in his father's presence, and perhaps that was the best way to survive this newest torture. For he knew, no matter how much he might protest, no matter how desperate he was to escape, he would attend the ball as his father wished because his father was king and he was prince, and he was nothing if not dutiful.

But he refused to be complicit in his suffering, at least, he refused to plan or discuss his torment.

Kit did not stop at his room.

His guards knew better than to follow him. Barely four months since the healers pronounced him whole and he spent the better part of his days in the lists, the only peace he had when he swung a sword or released an arrow. His soldiers made the fighting worthwhile, never shirking their duty to provide a good battle for him. He knocked them down faster than they could swing at him. The anger and pain in his soul gave him strength. If he didn't worship his gods, he would have thought the Darkness had claimed him as its own, so great was the terror and destruction he sought to work. But he never hurt his men, took special care to train only, never unleash the full fury in his soul.

This was not a day for the lists.

The emotion had been riding him hard for the last few weeks, an emotion he didn't have a name for, something between abject depression and mindless need. He didn't know what it meant, but the sword wasn't enough now, and he needed to run.

He came to the stables, not waiting for a groom to saddle his horse before he led the stallion from the stall and jumped onto the beast's back. More and more lately, he'd taken to riding the poor beast without a saddle, not wanting to take the time or explain where he was going to any groom or soldier sent to stalk him. He needed to move, and Oberon had never unseated Kit, always a steady mount to ride on.

"Fly, boy."

The horse responded to the command with a giddy hitch, sidestepping once before finding the path and sprinting down the lane. Hooves clacked over the bricked road, but Oberon had no trouble navigating the terrain, not even a slip on the slick surface. Kit should have waited to let the beast loose until they were beyond the city walls, but the moment the horse galloped, the thoughts deserted him for the feel of the wind in his face, hair whipping around his head. Shouts echoed at his back, but he ignored them, knowing the guards sent as his escort would follow his trail eventually, find him wherever the horse's head took him.

He closed his eyes, hands buried in the horse's mane, knees tight around the flanks, bent low over the neck. Kit tipped his face forward, hiding from the sunlight along the path. As much as he hated the elves, he found a quiet peace beneath the overhanging branches of the trees, the leaves that hushed the sounds of the world around him.

How long it took to get to the woods, he didn't know, but he didn't open his eyes until his horse's hooves no longer clicked over the road but clomped mutedly on thick ground beginning to burst with spring grasses.

An early ripening of the earth.

Spring come early, summer burns, the leaves will fall beneath a blanket of snow.

What Kit recalled of the past year was a mellow winter and a mild sun during Vellim and V'roshar. This winter would not be so easy to bear if the adage held true. There would be snow and cold and more like than not the harvest would suffer from the heat of the summer sun.

He would not regret the heat of this day, nor the advent of the spring as he sat up on Oberon's back and watched the woods close in around them.

The horse picked his path with care, winding through trees, snuffling at the few remaining patches of snow lightening the ground. Were they close enough to the Woodland realm that elves were watching him through the trees? Would said same elves hold true, let him pass unmolested through their forest? He almost hoped they wouldn't. The two knives he carried would hold against a sword. He'd gotten rather good with the short blades, good enough that he'd made Eli—

He didn't finish the thought. Every time he thought of her, he forcibly changed subjects. It was hard enough to bare her absence without seeing a reminder of her in his every action.

"*Even the Dienobolos have promised to send represent-atives*," he mocked his father's words.

Yes, send the elves to the palace walls, cage them in the glum of sandstone and marble boxes. No peace would come from the visit. No elf would take comfort in the cold sterility of the castle.

Yes, of course not including her, she was always the bloody exception to the rule.

He argued with his subconscious, letting the tirade consume him.

A river of thoughts, memories he'd forced down for nigh unto fifteen months now, almost a full year, of commanding himself not to think of the woman he lost.

But she was there, in the turn of Oberon's head, like the beast was looking in the shadows for her slight presence to call him towards. The birds sang overhead, and he expected to hear her shrill whistle scaring them off any moment. A branch touched his shoulder when he didn't duck far enough to avoid the caress, and he reached behind him, trying to bring her closer, take her hand in his own to hold as they rode.

She'd hated the palace walls as much as any elf.

Her windows were always wide open within her rooms, the fresh scent of all her plants encompassing the space. She pretended she was in her homeland, and he had taken the same comfort within her nest as she had.

He'd refused to return to her rooms once he woke from the coma.

He refused to allow them to be cleaned and reassigned.

During the war, she'd foregone a tent on the battlefield, preferring to spend the nights beneath the stars even when the weather was harsh and the enemy was too close to their lines for comfort. She'd slept in his bed when she needed the comfort of his arms to draw her back from the Darkness, and he'd come to her for the same. It had been natural to spend a night in a lake with her and no walls to confine them.

No wonder then that no matter where he went he felt her presence like a ghost around him.

And he wanted a lake right now. If he couldn't have her, he wanted the memory of a lake where he could pretend she was there holding him while he slowly sank under the water.

The temptation to simply breathe in the wet would be too great though.

Oberon shied, shuffling on the path, rearing so that only the tight grip of Kit's legs around its middle kept him seated.

Kit clenched his hands in the mane as he stared over the horse's head at the cloaked figure before him. Small, which Kit knew meant little in determining gender, but he still pegged the sprite as female. Elves were often more delicate of frame than their human cousins. "Have you come to tell me to leave your forest?"

The hood swayed left then right.

"No, then?"

A nod this time.

Kit laughed, a harsh sound that broke the silence around him. "Was there something you needed, or are you content to silently stare at me?"

He sat atop his mount, his hands sweating where they were buried in the horse's mane, prepared to reach for his knives if he needed to, force the beast to run if the woman proved violent towards him, if others should appear.

A gloved hand emerged from the billows of her cloak, waving him towards her. He caught a glimpse of light clothing, not enough to tell if she wore breeches or skirts as she turned away, expecting him to follow. He found he wanted to. How strange. He didn't mind this invasion of his solitude.

Oberon walked forward, quickly catching up with her smaller steps. The beast nuzzled her hood, and her hand rose to keep the dark green weave atop her head. Black strands blew in the slight wind, jostled free from his horse's ministrations. For a moment the pit in his soul had filled, thinking that, perhaps, somehow, she'd survived whatever death her people had prescribed for her. But he did not recognize her black hair, and she could not be the woman he hoped for.

Her hand stroked over Oberon's neck while they walked.

She made no complaint that he did not dismount to walk beside her or offer her his seat. Her stride never changed though to him they walked for hours. His eyes drifted closed and blinked slowly open, the healed body still not at the same stamina as Kit had once been. Her hand moved to his thigh, patting him as gently as she did the horse, afraid he was as skittish. The thought made him smile.

It was in a fog that his horse stopped. Not a visible fog, but one that had clouded over Kit's eyes, cast the world as part of a dreamscape, one he did not wish to remove himself from.

She supported him as he dismounted, her arm moving to circle his waist while his legs adjusted to bearing his weight once more. Where she led him, he followed. The longer they walked between the tightly spaced trees, the more he leaned on her, felt her leaning on him. It would be pleasant to draw her into his arms for a while, sleep in a bower of leaves and pretend that the arms around him actually cared, weren't pushing him back to a palace and the life of a prince who wished to be something simpler. An archer, perhaps. "Or a cloth weaver."

Had he spoken aloud? He couldn't tell, and he didn't care but that didn't stop his lips from quirking at the words.

He smiled at the woman. If she noticed, she gave no sign and it didn't truly matter, not when she pulled at his shirt and deftly stripped him of his boots then pants.

Funny, but she stripped him and he made no move to stop her. He didn't feel scarred standing so bared. Mayhap the advent of the hood kept him from noticing her gaze along the fading lines across his torso and back. They were white now, though the skin still stretched and pulled with his every movement.

She pressed her palm to his chest, the mark over his left side where the arrow had left its scar. Her fingers brushed over the mark, ran the ridges of it, brushed like she could smooth the scar away.

She did not touch him as his healers did. It must be the gloves she wore that made her more bold, her touch less intrusive against his skin. He should require all those seeking to caress his flesh to wear gloves so that he could not feel the trembling of shock from their fingers, nor the bareness of soft caresses over harsh weal.

He should care that he stood before a stranger naked as he hadn't been since he was born. He refused to think on the other times he'd been as naked as now.

Her touch was not for his flesh though. He had the impression that she stared through him, looked deeper, beneath his skin to what remnants of his soul remained. Words lingered on his tongue, wanting to tell her it was gone, long gone with the woman who it belonged to, but he held his tongue, let her touch the outer shell of what remained of the man within.

He could not understand the words that fell from her lips. The voice that spoke them though were far too similar, the alto as deep as another voice he remembered, another hurt he wished could be forgotten.

He trembled, the spell around him breaking the longer she touched him, clearing the fog as his mind fought to break free of memory and comfort.

Her hood tilted back, too deep for him to see the eyes he thought tried to catch his.

She stepped away.

He sighed, let the fog engulf him once more.

A tilt of her head, and he looked towards the pool lingering in the shade of a small grove. It was only natural for Kit to take the hand that she extended towards him, let her lead him to the water, the silence of the forest soothing.

She released him at the shallows, stepped away like she was afraid he would pull her in with him though the thought had not occurred before then, and made him laugh to see her retreat. If a faceless woman could smile, she did so, and he found himself smiling with her.

He stepped into the water, expecting to feel the winter cold biting at his toes, but it was warm, as warm as a nice bath at the palace, more soothing in its lack of confines.

Smooth stone was beneath his feet, not mud. This basin was not an idle pond deep in the woods as he'd thought. Should he leave? Was this a sacred sight of the Dienobolos? He found he didn't care.

The deeper he walked into the pool, the more the fog closed in around his mind, and the clearer his dreams became. Even knowing he was enchanted, he felt no fear at the magic and let it work its will on him. He looked over his shoulder, and she nodded again, permission or acceptance, an emissary of the forest or a child of its people, he took her word and relaxed within the warmth.

Kit dunked his head beneath the water, sluicing the liquid from his face when he remerged. He slicked his hair back along his scalp, blinking back the droplets weighing down his eyelashes.

He turned to watch her lift now bare fingers to the clasp at her throat, pull back the hood of her cape, draw the heavy weight aside and lay it on the ground at her feet. She settled in her skirt along the material, the light coloring in stark contrast to the deep greens of the forest around them. Had her feet always been bare, toes digging into the dirt at the edges of the cape? She blushed at his observation, and he grinned, stepping to the side of the pool, close enough to where she sat that a simple stretch allowed him to shift the hem of her cape over her feet to keep her warm. He squeezed her toes, and she wriggled beneath his touch.

"I miss your eyes most, Eli."

She smiled at him, waved him away and back into the pool where the winter chill couldn't touch him.

"Are you going to remain there?"

Her lips grinned wider, eyes sparkling in his imagination where the vision existed.

"I miss your voice."

But she did not speak to relieve that ache.

"Come with me."

Her smile turned sad. The glimmer in her eye was not that of the light's reflection but of moisture beading at the corner, a blink sending the shimmering tear down her cheek.

If he reached for her, he could wipe the small droplet from her face, brush away the second and third tears slipping down her porcelain skin.

He remained still, not touching her as she did not touch him.

She shook her head no.

He did not ask her why.

Kit stepped back into the deeper waters, dropping her gaze to search for a natural seat in the small pond, sinking into the steaming bath until the warmth covered his shoulders and he leaned his head against a soft piece of earth. He closed his eyes to her vision, would have covered his ears with his hands if she spoke, no longer wanting to see the vision, no longer wanting to be caught in a fantasy he could not have.

His skin pruned.

The leaf distilled sunlight waned over his head

Birds chirped in their green bowers. A deer or a fox scampered in the underbrush, disturbing the silence that had lingered around him.

The fog in his mind began to clear.

He opened his eyes and he was alone in the pool.

He should worry that he'd wandered onto some sacred spring of the Dienobolos. Perhaps, if he did not long so dearly for death, he might have been more concerned.

Kit slipped from the steaming water to retrieve his clothes, folded neatly in a pile beyond the pool's edge. A bath sheet was draped carefully over a low hanging branch at his boots' side.

He dried. He dressed. He followed the darkened path through the trees, a path he didn't remember but for the hand leading him though he followed it ably enough now.

His horse snorted at the other end of the tunnel, and whinnied when Kit finally appeared. The beast lowered himself to the ground, no vaulting onto the animal's back this time. Kit patted the stallion's head, and once more gave the roan its lead to return them to the palace.

Soldiers stirred on the roadside when he emerged from the trees. They looked as unconcerned as he felt, though they formed up around him quickly enough. Not a one dared to tell him he was a fool or that he was inconsiderate for having run off so uncaringly. Marius would have made the comment and then taken Kit to the lists the next morning to hammer the point home. Kit couldn't bring himself to care if he worried the men or not. He wanted to wallow in the mellow of the pool for a moment longer, let himself be distracted from all that laid before him, the ball, his father, the elves and his fate, remember the vision in the trees, not the truth of his life.

They reached the city gate as the sun set.

No one stopped him from leaving his horse with the groom and moving towards the palace without the entourage which had followed him.

Kit ascended the stairs to the great hall, followed it to the family dining room and his father waiting within.

The doors opened. The doors closed. Leon stood, a hand raised no doubt to berate Kit, but Kit spoke first, ignoring tradition to have his say.

"This will be the last ball, Father. At the end of the three nights, you will choose a bride for me. I will wed her. I will bed her. You'll have an heir you don't pity and are not afraid of," *and*

I'll be free of this life you wish me to live. The last he did not speak aloud, though it hung heavy in the air all the same.

His father made to reply, and Kit raised a hand to stop him, unfinished with his ultimatum.

"We both know I am no longer fit, Father."

Poor Leon, poor Kit, for the king did not dispute the words, sank slowly into his chair to which Kit came and knelt at his side.

"Surely you have thought the same over this past year."

"You are a prince." Which neither confirmed nor denied the truth of Kit's declaration.

Kit snorted but there was no humor in the sound. "I am a damaged prince. Who would want me to become a king someday?"

"Kit—"

Just his name.

His father said only his name, and Kit heard the pain and torment in the old man's voice, the tragedy weighing the sovereign down. He knew what Kit had suffered. Someone had told him that Kit might never be the man he was before. There was an acceptance of Kit's words in that single name that Kit had not expected to ever hear.

And he was profoundly grateful for his father's compassion.

"You will remain? You will aid whoever is to become king after me?"

Not a command. A plea from a parent losing his only child.

"You would want me to?"

"Always, Christophe. You are my son."

Kit swallowed, fought the closing of his throat and the despair at having no place to go regardless. "For as long as I can." *Until I can stand it no more.*

Three
The Four Hundredth and Eighty-Eighth Ball
The First Night

H
e refused to wear the red.

Kit didn't care if red was his father's chosen court color, or that blue went well with his eyes, or that gold would make the black of his hair all that more vibrant. He refused any and all colors of doublets the costumiers brought him, maintaining that he would wear the black already in his wardrobe and that they could waste their fripperies on the other nobles in attendance.

"But at least let us embellish it," they pled, and he stared back at them, unmoved until he was left alone with his severely cut jacket and the black breeches and boots to finish the ensemble.

He'd consented to having his boots shined to a bright sheen, accepted the circlet they'd demanded he wear.

His father wore a gold crown, as befit the ruling monarch. Kit wore silver, and rarely at that.

Never before had he worn the circlet for the ball, and yet his father insisted, and Kit couldn't find a good enough reason to argue against the demand.

So he wore the damn crown, and even consented to a the heavy silver chain, jewels of black onyx set between the small detailed crests of his ancestors: a bull, one leg raised as it prepared to charge for his greatest grandfather Euridone who gathered the first plains men into one village during a snowstorm; a griffin cradling a maiden in its arms for Marcel, the king who offered his life to the gods in payment for his people's survival from famine. His father bore the crest of a noble steed, he who unto the world opened, for Leon had established the roads, built over the crumbling foundations of what once was and opened trade to the westerners and those across the wide sea.

He touched the emblem of the wolf prowling in the woods.

His uncle's sigil, still honored as kin though the sight made Kit choke.

Once, when Kit was young, he'd asked the bastard why Kravn chose a lone wolf as his emblem, and his uncle had said it was to remember that he was not a king, that he roamed alone, but a wolf was always meant to be pack, and someday would return to Leon's side as such.

Kit's hand curled around the state chain. It took all he had not to rip the jewels from his throat, take sword and slice against the damned silver and onyx until it was no more.

He did not have a sigil on the chain.

His father threatened to denote Kit as the phoenix.

Kit forced his hand to open and let the heavy metal fall back against his chest, the black of his silk jacket all that kept the jewelry from touching his skin.

Three days, and he would have a bride. There would be a wedding. He would bed the poor lass. He would breed an heir. He wished only that the path of his life did not feel as dim as it did when he thought of what laid before him.

At the very least, he swore that he would protect whatever seed sprang from him. There would be no curse placed upon its head. No god would claim his child. Kit would not let them.

"The Arqueanmen are sending their princess. You would be heir to two thrones.

"Ignobis of the Quiofol is coming himself and bringing with him twelve of his virgin brides, all said to love dancing more than anything else. You would have the choice among them, which to take as your own. He's even offered one as a mistress to cement the binding of our two nations together as one.

Words spoken over the course of weeks trying to decide whom Kit would prefer as wife, to get anything resembling interest to spark in Kit's eye. His father had spoken of every woman who would attend, and Kit had sat and listened without care, because he truly didn't.

"The Priestosolos is coming herself to the ball, Christophe. The Piestosolos! She never leaves the woods, and she's bringing three Daughters with her. Well, of course, we'll choose one of the elves. We do owe them for everything and—"

Ah yes, a debt to be repaid for the murder of one of their own and his attempted murder over the course of his life. But, yes, let's reward them for saving a broken soul.

"You said you would marry whomever I chose."

Yes, and except for the irrational anger in his heart, he didn't regret granting his father that power. And at least an elf might know where she was buried, would be able to show him to the grave where he could lie on the ground and be close to her even as he was husband to another of her kind.

Kit adjusted the cuffs of his coat, the silly frilled shirt that peaked from the edges of the black, a dark grey, different enough to lend some color to his dress, if grey could be considered a color. The leather belt wrapped twice around his hips, the first loop tight, woven through the hoops at his waist, the second loop looser, able to bear the weight of the ceremonial sword he buckled to his left side. The scabbard was ceremonial. The sword was edged, a thin steel, lighter than the blade with the elaborately gilded hilt that was unwieldy where this blade was uncompromising. He hadn't worn that formal blade since he nearly died with it in his hand, and it'd taken a girl to save his life. He smiled at that thought, that he should wear a real weapon lest he chase after some other pool fool wise enough to run to the woods away from him. The smile died, because he would not be chasing the woman he wanted.

At least he'd be able to protect himself without her aid.

How many times had she leaned in his doorway, ready to escort him to the ball, or to a formal event, and said the same to him?

He'd worn the green jacket for her. She'd insisted only the once, and he'd done it, and then his world had ended.

The green was still in his wardrobe. When the healers left and his frame was bone and flesh and his father commissioned a new set of clothes for him, he hadn't let them take that one coat that he would never wear but couldn't abide losing.

He turned from the sight, back to his bed and his weapons laid atop the mattress.

A dagger at his hip, gilded sheath to adhere to the strictures of the ball, one in his boot that no one need known about.

A final glance in the mirror at his pale face and his sweat beaded forehead.

Who would have thought that a prince could look so sick of a dance?

With a dignity he didn't feel, he stepped from his room to the flitty laughter of noble women walking through the halls just past the royal apartments on their way to the ballroom or the banquet room or some other such room opened for the masses for these three interminable days. He followed sedately enough behind the guards posted outside his room, so that he couldn't run? Or there to protect him from the women who would conveniently get lost at the edge of dawn and seek a way to entangle him in wedlock without his choice? As his father had said, the choice was already made, now was just a matter of actually taking his vows. Three hundred and eighty-seven years and he'd had her in his arms, had the ring in his pocket, and he'd been too late. Three hundred and eighty-eight years, and he'd missed his chance. If an heir wasn't expected of him, he would go to his death never having touched a woman in a carnal light, been happy to have found her on the other side of the void, pure for her.

His breath hitched.

But then, he wasn't really *pure* anymore, was he? Not after...

This was all too soon, and his heart was hammering, and his palms were sweating through the gloves he tugged on when he left his chambers.

Losing himself in the darkness of his mind, he'd done it once, found his way back from it once, could do it again if he needed to. He could be whatever his father demanded of him. All he had to give up was the man he was, become an *it* once again. The kit, not—

"My prince?"

He'd stopped walking, and now one of the soldiers was holding his arm, standing far too close.

"Apologies. I was lost in my thoughts."

Could they hear the lie? That it wasn't thoughts of the ball that he was lost in but darker, crueler remembrances?

"Are you ready to continue, my lord?"

It's "Your Highness." He was not a lord. He was higher than a lord. And all he wanted was to just be a man, not a count or a duke or a sir or a lord, just a man, a baker or a soldier or a tailor might be nice.

He didn't tell the guard that though. With a small nod of his head, a "Yes, please," he motioned for the men to precede him, followed them to the royal entrance to the ballroom, waves of sound, musicians tuning their instruments, gossips tittering away waiting for him to arrive, buffeted the small space he stood in as he waited for the steward to announce him and for his hell to begin. He adjusted his gloves. The left hand curled over the hilt of his sword, the right was stiff against his thigh.

The crowd quieted at his fanfare and the steward gave Kit a nod before walking out onto the balcony and announcing Kit's name. His guards lined the stairway. Kit stepped out and bowed.

CR&O

"Princess Aurora, it is my greatest honor to introduce you to my son, Christophe."

"Might I have this dance, your highness?"

The slight woman looked nervously to her escort for confirmation before nodding her head and taking Kit's extended hand. She was as unhappy to be here as was he. That made him feel lighter about the whole of the situation, though he doubted his jaded response would please his father.

They danced well together to a reel and then a Gavotte. He managed to coax a smile to her pale lips when he stumbled and bumped into a preening man who kept staring at the princess with a mix of disdain and desire. Anytime the man's gaze caught Aurora's, she blanched, and Kit took issue with his partner's distress.

When the waltz began, she graciously took his hand, though there were others ready to take his place, her place, by that point. He obliged the slight girl, for she was slight and young, even by her people's years, too young to be considered a woman yet.

"You will not marry me, will you, Prince?"

He smiled at her frankness, finding something to like about the woman she would become. "No, your Highness."

"There are shadows in your eyes, shadows that hide much sorrow."

He spun her, not knowing how to respond.

"I cannot lift those shadows for you. I'm not sure I should try, though I would be a friend, if you needed one."

"I have a plethora of friends gathered round, your high-ness."

"Not the type of friend many of these women would be." Her gaze snaked to the people around them, reptilian in move-ment, a product of her heritage. Kit had not had many dealings with the dragons before, their country rather closed though his father had ridden to meetings with them over the years. Too dan-gerous for Kit to go, of course, but the woman before him did not appear dangerous, and her smile was a softer thing than what many of the courtesans wore.

"You are too young to be so wise, Princess."

She smiled at him, though her eyes darkened with acknowledgment. Not many must see the truth of the woman they saw.

Kit wondered if all dragons were the same.

"The flesh is young, yes." He met her mahogany gaze, so dark within the candlelight of the ballroom. "The soul is far older indeed."

He could not tell if it was a rebuke or simple statement of fact. "Forgive me, my lady." He bowed his head while he held her in his arms, this ancient soul in the body of a youth. It put him to shame, having thought her but a girl, and for that he apologized and had the feeling she knew it.

"Nothing to forgive, Prince. Your soul is much different than the body you bear too."

"Too true, your highness." Too true.

The song ended, and he bowed again, ensuring that his was the motion of deepest respect, that those around him recognized that whoever this princess was, she was to be most honored.

She smiled demurely back at him, allowing him to lead her to her guardians standing along one wall of the great chamber. "I will be gone in the morning, though I would not insult you or your father by my leave taking."

His father would say she was too young, and the slight would be easily forgiven as such.

"No insult in the slightest."

Indeed, his father might approve that the youth left early and was not saddened when she failed to catch herself a prince. Of course, she was not an elf, and had no chance regardless.

Still, Kit found the woman pleasant and would be sad to see this ancient young princess leave.

They would have been a poor match, this girl with a woman's eyes and a woman's secrets. Too much swirled in the coffee gaze, hinting at the power and love she held or would hold for another someday. He did not want to come between that, wouldn't.

She extended a hand and he kissed the back of her white glove, pressed his forehead to the fabric as a sign of admiration to her.

"Thank you, Prince. I had not thought to find any joy here." Her fingers touched his jaw, turning his gaze to meet hers. "The Gods…they say all things return in time. Perhaps your time is come, young one."

He smiled at the term, even as her guards shifted steps, wondering at the exchange, unsure how he would take it. "I do not believe in the gods, my lady. They've brought me only sorrow."

"A pity, for they have believed in you, and a wiser choice they could not have made."

CR&Ω

"Lord Ignobis, please, please, bring your fair maidens here to meet the prince."

King Leon waved at a hulky giant of a man, his head at least two taller than Kit's own tall build.

Staring up at the man craned Kit's neck back. Ignobis, skin sunburned a dark red, hair shaved short to his round head, stepped before the king and took up nearly the entire dais with his bulk.

Kit had not been made to feel small in—

Few sought to overpower him, and yet this man did so with nothing but his size. It was unnerving, and brought back far too many memories. Kit's breath held in his chest even as he bowed to the man before him.

A gaggle of women stood behind the man, guarded by as many giants each. Ignobis kept his wives pristine, in body and mind, or so it seemed. Not a one of them took their eyes from the floor to look at Kit when the lord started listing off names. They stood still, unmoving, like they were afraid of drawing the noble's attention even as they knew they must have it.

Did they think it would be a mercy to be Kit's bride rather than their husbands?

Still untouched.

The thought flitted across his mind, and Kit looked again at these cowering, browbeaten women and felt pity stir in his breast for them. Even if they were not now at the hands of their husband, Kit saw the marks of long horror in their sallow skin and sullen faces. Whatever life they held with the man who claimed them, it was not a merciful one, and stirred memories far too dark in Kit's mind.

"Go, go, you must dance with them."

His father laughed when Ignobis stepped aside and opened the way for Kit to reach the women. Kit could not tell one sunken face from another. He did not wish to dance with any of them. He did not want them to know he had nothing but sorrow to heap upon them nor only pity for their plight.

He extended his hand, and the women stepped aside, the slowest left to join him for the first dance.

A quadrille, minuet, Loure and Gigue, Bourrée, Gavotte and Musette and the orchestra called for a brief pause and Ignobis claimed his brides saying there were three more nights to choose during.

Pearl clung to Kit's arm when her husband came to retrieve her. She looked over Kit's shoulder at the line of her sisters he'd yet to partner with, Ruby and Sapphire, Topaz and Garnet, begging them to save her from her master's touch. Kit held her hand until Ignobis pulled her sharply away and it would have caused a scene to hold any longer.

Her sister wives followed slowly behind her retreating form. None fought against the demands of their husband.

"I am sorry."

Diamond stopped and looked at him.

He thought she might speak, might beg, might curse, but she said nothing, her eyes dead as she turned back to her sisters and followed the lordling from the room to wherever he was staying within the palace for the ball.

Kit could not save just one or two of them. He wasn't sure he would turn out any better than their bastard husband when he wed regardless. With a fervent prayer to the gods that the women wouldn't suffer, he returned to his seat beside his father's throne and watched the brightly dressed men and women of the court dance and gossip while he waited for his next partner to arrive.

CR80

In her face he saw the woman he loved grown older, grown wiser, and he hated it.

The Priestosolos walked steadily up the steps of the dais, and inclined her head at the king, her gaze raking Kit without caution, beyond protocol. He met her steely eyes, and forced himself not to snarl at the strongest elf of the Dienobo-los. His hands clenched on the armrests of his chair.

"You've healed well, Prince Christophe. I'm glad to see my talents were not wasted on you."

He clenched his teeth, knowing he should state his gratitude for her healing, knowing that any words that left his mouth would curse the woman before him.

"And what talents they are, Priestosolos. You honor us with your presence. It is because of you and your skill that we are here at all."

Her gaze broke from Kit's and she looked at his father with a gentle smile turning her lips at the compliment. They exchanged pleasantries, his father's rasping tenor mellowed against her soft mezzo. With his eyes closed, Kit could almost pretend that the woman was any other person speaking with his father than the one who had placed a bounty on his head the moment he was born, and who'd killed her own daughter for the saving of his life.

Because that's who Eli was, wasn't it? She was the daughter of the Priestosolos. Not the daughter in the way the three women cloaked in black were Daughters of the Wood, but by flesh and blood and heart. And didn't the realization make sense? Eli's coldness, the strength of her spirit to withstand the life of an assassin with compassion intact? The knowledge that she'd never hid, and he'd never asked for before

And this woman who was priest and healer had still had not hesitated to order an infant killed, her own daughter murdered.

And the three fake Daughters at her back were here to be his bride, and his father was content with the choice. Kit should be grateful it wasn't the bitch himself he was being pledged to.

"Come forward."

The three women answered their priestess' command, stepping away from the crowd and to the edge of the dais, never taking the steps up, always remaining below Kit and his father and their mistress. They pulled their dark hoods down, revealing hair the color of corn spun silk, a red as dark as blood, and one as dark as a moonless night. Their faces were masked, golden ovals obscuring any question of bone structure beneath, a mesh over the eyes so that he could not see the color behind the disguise. All three wore gowns as dark as the Darkness they worshipped, draping gowns that reached to the floor, covering them from head to toe, their hands gloved, their throats shadowed. They were of similar shapes, all of a height. And they were here to wed him, and he had to fight not to flinch from their appearance.

He dismissed the blond and redhead out of hand, not knowing why his gaze was drawn to the raven haired elf, ignoring the shiver of memory, not wanting to remember that day in the woods, the dream of a dead woman.

Kit had the impression that she was studying him as much as he studied her, though he could tell nothing with the mask over her face.

She was, if he was honest, perhaps not as well-endowed as her sisters. The black of her dress clung with more ceremony to her slenderer curves, the hint of muscles beneath. Not a daughter of Pirie then. Perhaps this sister walked the forests, worshipped the aspect Ashet and the fields and furrows between the tress. He would be amused if he thought the Priestosolos would dare to send a sentinel of Echi as a bride for him. Already one of the Assassin's brethren had died for him. He would find no comfort in another of their ilk.

The one he stared at shifted, her head bowing slightly at his continued appraisal.

That it was noted was not lost on him.

He subjected each of the other two to the same perusal, remembering not to turn his gaze back to her lest his unmasked face give him away.

Silence broke him from his thoughts, his head turning to his father and the priestess to meet their stare.

"Ask them to dance, son."

The conductor motioned for a recess.

"The first set after the break is yours, my ladies."

Not a one answered him, a nod, and then they moved into the crowd, the black of their dresses setting them apart from the colorful menagerie of the guests around them.

"You did not listen to a word I said to the priest."

"Did I need to?" He met his father's gaze. "You said the choice was made, Father. I assumed my input was not further required. Or did I miss a question directed at me whilst you spoke with," he bit his tongue, "the priestess?"

The older man flushed red in anger but recovered quickly enough. The blush could be put down to the color of his coat though Kit doubted anyone had seen the man's face. "Perhaps you would be interested to know that your future bride is bound in silence until the stroke of midnight on the third night of the ball?"

"Not really."

Leon sputtered, his hand gripping Kit's shoulder with a strength Kit found impressive given that he thought his father little more than a politician. "For the gods' sake, Kit. Try! I do not want you to suffer in whatever marriage you would have."

"I would not have one."

"You swore—"

"So choose, Father. I don't care. If the witches would prefer their silence, then I have no qualms with it. The dance floor is no place for discussion anyways."

"Kit…if you prefer the Princess Aurora or one of Ignoblis' offerings, I would not stop you from picking them. I would have you pleased, my son."

He could not tell his father that his son was dead inside. The son they'd brought back from the woods, carted in a coma through the trees, from a dark tower, was nothing more than a ghost of the man he'd once been. Oh yes, he knew others suffered harsher fates than himself. He knew it was only a sense of entitlement that made him think he deserved to be treated with more care, as better than any other man out there. He didn't even know if the man he'd come upon in the forest before his capture had been recovered, recognized and buried and hailed a hero for all that he suffered. Was it bad to comfort himself with the thought that perhaps the poor fool had not suffered as long as Kit? He hoped it was so at least. And in the end it meant nothing, and he had no response for his father but silence.

"The musicians return, and I am to dance, my king." Kit bowed, crossing his arm over his chest in the formal way a courtier would acknowledge their king. He bowed, and did not look at his father's face as he descended the dais and extended his hand, not caring which of the black robed women accepted the offering, just that someone accepted and he could pretend, for a moment, that it was another black dressed woman who swayed in his arms.

CR℘

He knew he danced with all three of them. Vaguely, he remembered the change in songs, the change in grips clutching at his hand as they twirled around the ballroom. He bowed, his partner changed, and he remained on the dance floor, refusing to return to his father's side, preferring to lose himself to the dancers whom he hated.

Silks pressed against his legs, reds and blues and golds, and he let the hordes pull him into their masses, sticking out in his black, always visible, always known as different amidst the colors. He smiled politely to each partner. He even managed a few pleasant, rather trite, remarks. Yes, the weather was indeed very mild for this time of year. No, he didn't think the frosts would return to ruin the spring blooms. Indeed, he hoped the adages were false and that the coming winter was not too harsh. Practically a year away, and still they talked of winter and weather and colors and carriages. Nothing pertinent, inane chatter, not a mind among those who found their way to his arms.

He caught his father looking at him once, motioning to return to the thrones. He ignored the command and spun away, spun until his feet ached and beyond.

The bells chimed thrice, and the band played a final waltz, and Kit begged his leave of the peacock colored woman in his arms, smiling as he fled the ballroom in advance of the guests.

His guards could not catch him as he moved through the halls. They needn't have feared. He found his way to his rooms easily enough, locked the door at his back when he entered and shrugged out of his doublet, the gray shirt beneath sticking to his skin with sweat.

He ripped the cloth away, leaving it a puddled mess on his floor, kicking his boots off quickly after, the stockings covering his feet.

He stood at his balcony, bare-chested and barefoot, breathing shallowly of the crisp air, the sun too far away from dawn.

Those invited to stay in the palace for the length of the ball would rise late the next morning. Breakfast would be another affair of mind-numbing conversation and rhapsodic smiles aimed at him. Almost he looked forward to it, just to see if the elves would be uncovered or if they would retain their masks throughout their stay, dancing or not.

Like the elf standing in the courtyard below his balcony, leaning lightly against the rail to the garden.

He could not pick out her hair from the night around her.

The black harpy then.

What was it about her that drew him so, that he fought against the wanting of?

He found a white shirt in his wardrobe and slipped the silk over his head. He didn't bother with the ties at his throat or tucking the excess into his breeches. He didn't bother with stockings or boots, slipping through the small door that, upon a day, would lead to a second set of rooms for his wife and his children. He'd used the escape often as a child, never since he reached his majority though, always keeping the locks turned so that they could not be used against him either. The locks were on his side of the door. He slipped through the rooms and down the far stairwell, found his feet eating up the ground, arms pumping at his sides, running across the stones, running to the woman on the terrace, stumbling to a halt before the glass doors to the outside.

She hadn't moved from her position except to tilt her head back, her long black tresses hanging down her spine in curling waves, blowing lightly in the breeze.

He remembered.

He remembered finding a similar woman escaping the harsh confines of a crowded ballroom and seeking sanctuary in a place silent from the noise above stairs. Another woman, and another ball, another life long ago.

But this was not that woman.

And he was not that boy.

The knife was in his hand before she had a chance to draw another breath. Not the elf standing in the garden. No, this was not that elf, who found him in the dark and who he reserved the majority of his hate for.

He did not hesitate to push the Priestosolos against the wall, covering her mouth to stall whatever words she sought to speak to him, any cry for help she might utter. She'd found him silently enough; she could die the same.

"I could kill you, and it would be an easy thing, not only in deed but in thought." His voice whispered in the still of the night, no one there to listen to him but the woman he held captive. "I would have gladly died to spare her life. This body would have gladly died, would not have cared what became of it so long as she lived, but you saved it. You saved me when you'd been trying to kill me from childhood. Was it that your assassin failed to kill me all those years ago? Or was it that she stayed and that is what you couldn't stand most, that she stayed with me and you lost a disciple and thought to punish me with this half-life while taking hers? And now you think I will be your tool, married to your spawn without a thought or care of my own?" He shifted closer to her, ignored the shaking in his hand as he shifted his free fingers to her dark hair, felt the supple softness of her skin beneath his fingers, tangled himself against her scalp and yanked, relishing the hiss of pain as she arced into his knife and drew a line of blood across her throat. "Which one do you not care to lose, priestess? Which one will you sacrifice to my hate?"

"You do not hate us."

He smiled, a cold, cruel smile that he pressed to her cheek, his words a whisper over her flesh. "Only you. Are you so willing to trust that my hate won't run cold enough to take my revenge on your Daughters?"

"You do not hate my daughter."

"You have no daughter, bitch." He released her, stepping back, eyes scanning the hall, noticing that the gold masked woman now stared at the window where he stood with his knife, barefoot and his shirt gaping at his throat, frantic and wild and without anywhere or anyone to run to.

A younger him would have been horrified.

When he woke in the morning, after a night of fitful sleeping with memories of his actions to rouse him, he would be horrified.

Now, now he opened the door, ignoring the elf panting in the hallway and crossed the distance between himself and her successor.

He held the knife between them, the blade pointed towards the ground, dripping red rubies onto the broken stone path.

She gripped his wrist, steadying his hand.

With a calm grace, she turned the blade towards her chest, stepping into the point, enough to pierce the black of her dress, bare the pale flesh beneath as the edge cut the lace of her gown and stained her skin with her mother's red.

They stood there, staring at each other while he imagined another woman's eyes and the black covered pools of the present begged him to forget.

"Will the debt be paid?" *If I kill you... Will I find peace if I take your life for the one you destroyed?*

Her gloved fingers left his wrist, brushed over his lips in a gentle caress, akin to the first tasting of a fine wine. It was only natural to purse said flesh and press against her thumb.

Her chest rose and fell faster and he pulled the knife away in fear of piercing her pale, pale skin.

He replaced the knife in its sheath at his hip, turned and walked away, into the hallway, past the woman still standing there, watching, up the stairs and down the hall to his rooms, ignoring the commotion of his guards as they tried to figure out how he sped past them. He waited for them to unlock his door before slipping into his darkened rooms and closing himself away.

He sank against the wood, sank to the floor and wrapped his arms around his upraised knees, ignoring the way his sword dug into his side, and the dagger slipped loose from his hip.

Kit leaned his head against his knees and closed his eyes.

What had he done?

Why did he care?

Four
The Four Hundredth and Eighty-Eighth Ball
The Second

‧

He plead exhaustion to escape brunch the next morning. The ladies of the court were excused from other activities as they went about the arduous process of preparing themselves for the festivities of the night to come. The men went on a short hunt through the manicured lawns of the estate.

No one expected him to join in that, the memories that it might conjure for him.

That they thought him so fragile would have made him growl or laugh, he wasn't sure, seeing as it was likely true regardless.

He slipped from his rooms and the expression on his face must have been adequate enough to convince his guards to let him be, wander as he would without their presence guarding him. One thing to be grateful for, he supposed, though there were few places left to explore within the palace grounds not invaded by some such frivolity or other. Women laughed and cackled in the parlors while they discussed dresses and which color it seemed Kit preferred since he'd dance with it so many times the night before. He only knew what they discussed because the screaming denials of pink and peach reached his ears and he investigated before he realized what it was the women were actually discussing.

The older gentlemen, not out on the hunt, took up residence in the library, stealing Kit's solace that he might have found among the many volumes of books housed within the wooden shelves.

The ballroom was abuzz with servants resetting candles and polishing windows and sweeping the floor.

The kitchens were too terrifying to imagine as Kit got as close to the stairs as he dared before the clanking and sizzling of pots and pans made him hurry away.

Soldiers were in the lists.

The duelists were all otherwise engaged for the day and their space occupied by dancing instructors anyways.

Kit stopped to breathe.

He hadn't felt at home in the palace since he returned bedridden. Likely before that too. The only place that felt like home to him was a heart no longer beating, no matter how much the midnight beauty made him ache inside.

Only one place remained touched by her influence.

Careful that no one saw him, he slipped from the palace steps towards the barracks, stopping at every sound lest someone should come towards him. He was undisturbed as he reached her rooms and slipped behind the unlocked door to her space. The leaves of her plants were vibrant against the sand-dun of the walls. Someone had watered her garden, cared for it even though she wasn't here. He walked through the plants, brushing aside leaves, fingers lingering over the waxy green stalks and brightly blooming spring blossoms towards her bedroom, the area she'd cordoned off with a drapery, a private place he'd found as much sanctuary in as she.

The sheets on her bed looked fresh changed, turned back as though she could slip beneath them at the end of any day. There was something of the forest here, deeper than just the flowery scent of fresh blooms, fresh turned earth, grass after a storm, leaves burning in the autumn fall.

He stripped his vest from his shoulders, unbuttoned the clasps of his shirt from his throat.

Kit hung the garments over the back of an old chair in one corner. He settled his boots beneath the seat and tread carefully over the wooden floors, warm compared to the rug covered stones of his room. He hesitated before pulling back the covers and slipping between the sheets. Did it disrespect her memory to lay in her bed absent her consent? Did he have it in him to care?

Strands of fabric wove a canopy over his head, the green vines growing out of velvets and laces and whatever other fabrics she'd scavenged to make the covering. Bunched fabrics resembling flowers were pinned to the mess, dipping towards the bed as though truly alive and she was the sun they reached for.

He blinked, staring up at the lime and fern and mint colored ropes above him. He blinked, and it took him longer to open his eyes when a shaft of sunlight pierced through the shade and landed against his face, warming his chilled body though he had the blankets pulled around him.

It was easy enough to draw one of the pillows beside him, wrap his arms across the soft fabric and pretend that he held something firmer, just as lush but in a different way, that the heat of a body was beside him and not this heat warmed mound of feathers and cloth. His father would be shocked to know Kit knew what it was like to hold a woman not his wife in his arms. But he'd been on a battlefield, and he hadn't wanted to hold another soldier when she came to him and asked and offered comfort.

He nuzzled the curve of neck in his arms, imagined the rise and fall of a chest against him, the pound of a heart against his fingertips.

We are not at war, Kit.

No, not on a battlefield, but always at war. This was just inside him now, hidden behind the flesh he bore.

She offered no more words inside his head.

Her silent, black haired sister sat beside him, the full face mask gone and only a piece of gold mesh covering her eyes remained. She took his hand from the pillow, lifting his arm aside so she could remove the piece of fluff from his dream, replace it with her own warm body. Her head burrowed beneath his chin, into his chest, lips a soft caress against his skin as she turned her face to the side and wrapped an arm around his waist and he wrapped her in his embrace.

She smelled like her sister, all earth and twilight, the edges of the dark.

He breathed her in, and gave himself to sleep.

ᘓᘔ

He smiled at the press of lips to his, the breath of wind across his face as he woke slowly to a setting sun.

How long had it been since he'd slept more than an hour or two at a time?

He replaced the pillow at the head of the bed, straightened the bedclothes when he stood, replacing the room to what it had been before he disturbed the dead. His fingers brushed along the top of the chair when he donned his clothing, slipped back into his boots.

The room looked untouched.

He wondered how many times he could sleep between her sheets before his scent overpowered hers and he lost that last touch of her in his life.

Would his wife mind that he spent his nights in a dead girl's rooms?

His lips twitched into a smile. He truly didn't care what some elf thought of him. He almost hoped that Eli'd left a curse on the place, that any of her sisters who dared enter the dwelling would incur some blasted stomach ache or night terrors of spiders biting at their skin.

He wished her plants a fine evening before he closed the door and left, fingers trembling over the latch now that he had committed himself to departure. Gods, how he wanted to stay and dared not remain a moment longer.

⊂⊃

A guard met him at the steps of the palace, looking him over for any injuries as the man hustled Kit to his chambers and a valet, uncalled for and unwelcomed, forced Kit to a bath, laying out clothing for him to wear despite Kit's protests that he could manage on his own.

At least the fool left him his blacks, and Kit slipped into the more loosely tailored coat over a white silk shirt and slacks that fell in neat pleats down his legs. He did not wear boots with the ensemble, slipping his feet into equally black half shoes that did nothing to detract from the hem of his garments.

He felt a fool in the clothing, but had seen enough men sporting the attire the night before to know it was the fashion.

He refused to think on how he'd acquired a set of the garments for himself, who had been close enough to measure him, the implied touching that must have occurred as such.

CЯЄↄ

Tonight was less formal.

He entered with a group of gentleman similarly aged, managing a few insipid conversations with them before they split to allow him to make the first bow before the king and step aside as they each took turns at subservience.

Aurora was, as promised, absent from the proceedings.

He noted this without his father's regard, quietly grateful that the lady had managed an escape he himself was forbidden.

The five wives of Ignobis he hadn't managed a dance with the night before returned for the second night of the ball, the other women absent from the proceedings. He took one dance with each lady and watched as they were hurried from the hall in the aftermath. It seemed the good lord didn't want Kit forming any attachments with the offered brides.

The sisters of the Dienobolos were in attendance, though only the flaxen haired lady and her ginger counterpart approached him for a dance. Tonight, their faces were covered in half masks dripping with silken veils to cover their cheeks and lips. Flashes of what they might look like behind the shadows tried to draw his eye, but he danced unseeing.

Their priestess was absent from the ball altogether.

Other dancers approached him after he'd done his duty by those guests given status for the event. Subtler gowns, gowns that draped rather than billowed, pressed against Kit during waltzes and reels. He could feel his partners' legs touching his own when they spun too close to him. As he recalled, he'd noticed a similar phenomenon the night prior with the elfin dresses of the Dienobolos. It appeared that if nothing else, the ladies of the wood were changing fashion, and the women of the ball were all too keen to change to suit the trend.

It mattered little to Kit what they wore or didn't wear for a dance.

Kit did not pretend enjoyment in the act this night.

He danced, as was expected of a prince, paid the proper courtesies and adoring glances.

Through it all, he wore a smile that was as fake as many of the jewels on these proper ladies' necks. No one called him on it, but everyone knew. That he was displeased was not new to the proceedings. Had he been cheery, likely the patrons would have been terrified and blubbered, wondering what new ailment afflicted their prince.

At the first break in music, he excused himself from the ballroom and made his way to the great hall where tonight's feast had been assembled. He took a glass of wine and a sweetmeat for himself, pleading introductions when he was begged to sit with this table or that. He managed a quiet moment in the hall, long enough to guzzle the red and swallow the sausage before a flock of young lasses exited the ballroom and he fled in the opposite direction of their approaching coven.

He found himself in a quiet music room, stopping the minstrel from plucking on his instrument with a raised hand. "You're dismissed, please."

The poor man fled Kit like he was Hades come to collect his soul.

If only Kit could flee as easily, he would not feel such a weight on his shoulders.

He sighed when the musician rushed past him and he locked the doors upon the man's exit, managing a small sigh in relief that he had found a haven to escape to.

Kit moved to take a seat on one of the lush couches of the room, wide enough to serve as a bed should he manage to stay hidden away long enough for silence to fill the halls.

He noticed her then, sitting in the corner, her hands folded in her lap, unconcerned with his presence or his subsequent dismissal of her entertainment. His fingers clenched over the edge of the couch. "My apologies, my lady. I had thought I was alone."

The troubadour hadn't looked at the woman to alert Kit to her presence, hadn't hesitated in leaving his audience behind at Kit's demand.

She didn't appear to mind the quiet.

Perhaps she was as desperate for solitude as he.

"And I apologize for last evening."

She nodded her head, and he caught sight of her lips behind the gauze, a delicate pink that contrasted sweetly with her moonlight skin.

"Would you remove your mask?"

She shook her head, though he had the impression that she smiled at his request, despite denying it.

"Your priestess is not in attendance tonight." He did not expect an answer, and was rewarded with her silence and what he felt was her stare. "I should like to extend my regrets to her for my actions previously."

The woman stood.

He'd not heard her name.

In truth, he didn't remember any of the three elves being introduced beyond title of Daughter.

He'd meant to ask Eli if that was there way, that they were called by their titles and stations rather than given a name to be known by. Did all "daughters," in turn serve Pirie? Eli had called the ones who attacked them by name, hadn't she? He'd not thought to look up the words she'd used back then, and now the words slipped through his memory without remembrance.

She approached him as she would a wounded animal, coming at him from the front, allowing him ample time to move aside, to keep her in his direct vision. It was habit that had him turning at an angle to her approach, allowing his peripheral to catch anything that might be at his back, attacking in tandem with her.

She stopped at his maneuver.

He did not apologize for it.

She extended both hands, her palms towards the arched ceiling overhead, clear of weapons. With a soft swish of her gown, she sat on the edge of his couch, turned so that her back was in the corner and she could watch him as he watched her. Her hands remained in her lap for him to see.

He recognized the motion as a request to join her.

He obliged, not taking his gaze from her masked face as he circled the back of the couch and sat against the opposite end, spine equally pressed into the meeting corner of cushions.

She made no other movements for long moments, allowing him to stare, and he sat wondering if she stared in turn. Slowly, so as not to startle him, she reached down to the edges of her skirts.

He tensed, waiting for a knife to slip into her hand and the lunge that would plunge the blade between his ribs. Would he seek to stop her if she attacked? He did owe her a debt of blood as he had cut her mistress the night before.

Her fabrics rustled, and there was a soft thump onto the carpeting, followed quickly by a second equally soft thud. She replaced her hand on the arm of the chair, moved the other to the back, and lifted herself enough to curl her legs beneath her bottom, settle her skirts around her calves so he could not see her covered feet, if elves wore stockings that is.

He glanced quickly at the shoes, expecting leaves and twigs bound together.

That wasn't fair, he knew that. Eli'd worn the same shoes as any other lady of the court. He had no right to think this woman would be different, and yet he thought it all the same.

Her shoes were as black as her gown, as black as the starless night beyond the castle walls. The crystal caught the light and refracted it, sparkling in the dimming candle flickers from chandeliers set to burn for too long. Remarkable shoes. Impossible shoes.

He held her gaze as he bent to lift one in his hand, bent close enough that her gown brushed against his arm and chest as he leaned into her and brought the slipper to his eyes to examine.

"Incredible."

He turned the slipper over between his fingers. Weightless, nigh lacking in any tactile sensation at all. It was like holding a piece of the Darkness given shape and form to suit the whim of the wearer but ready to return to its true nature at the flick of a hand.

"Best not to show these to any of the other women, my lady. Your dresses they might manage to emulate, but we've no magic such as this to call on for fair maidens to trample."

Her head tipped back and he had the impression she laughed with him. Back and tilted to the left. Another elf had similarly sat before.

He turned his eyes back to the shoe and the safety it represented. "Will you take vengeance against me if I close my eyes and took my gaze from you?" He looked at her long enough to watch the shake of her head, the hand that rose and begged him to lean back in what comfort he could find.

"Should I trust you?" He imagined another woman sitting across from him, a grin stretching her lips wide as she replied that he had before, why not once more? But it had taken many years for that other woman to gain his trust, and he was no longer that boy.

She leaned forward slowly, stopping when he tensed, shifting further when he relaxed at her approach. He raised a hand whether in warding or benediction he didn't know, but she took the gesture as her own, caught his fingers between hers. The white glove he wore pulled smoothly from his flesh. The grip she had on him did not allow for him to clench his fingers and pull away. He vibrated, the deer before the huntsman, and watched the black of her gloves melt away with the will of her magic.

She brushed her bare thumb across the back of his hand, the scars on his knuckles from fist fights in the barracks, a hard jab with unprotected skin. He sucked in a breath when she pressed too deeply against the still tender flesh from his most recent bout in the lists, but he did not stop her, and she did not pull away despite his discomfort. She stroked over the length of his fingers pulled from their fist with her gentle ministrations. He didn't offer any resistance when she turned his hand over and stared at the horror of his palm.

Kit turned his head aside, not wanting to see her reaction to the destruction that was his skin. The mottled skin was red and raised, extra padding that still ached and pulled with every flex of his fingers. She traced the edges of the cross, the way the longest beam extended to the base of his heart finger, over the crest of his wrist. The ring in the center of the design was a deeper red than the surrounding skin, highlighted in its exaggerated precision. This she traced with extra care, lingering over the mark though she, nor anyone, could know what it was from. That did not stop her touch from having more compassion when she stroked it. Maybe her magic gave her a knowledge he hoped to hide.

He flinched at the press of her nail into the skin. It brought his gaze back to hers, the mesh covered eyes that bored into him despite his inability to see them.

Yes, he still had feeling in his hands.

Yes, it was likely a product of her people's healing.

"Should I trust you?" The question slipped from his lips a second time, and he caught the straightening of her should, the hitch in her breath.

Was she nervous to be so interrogated? Was there something she wished to hide? Were memories crowding her the same as they crowded around him?

Her face tipped back to his hand, and he looked down to where she still held him. She traced the ring once more, slashed from left to right across his palm, two dots piercing the upper portion of the design. She wrote "yes," across his palm, and he smiled for she'd written the same many years ago when he'd asked after a letter in her barracks and the marks so different than his own alphabet.

Not her. This was not that woman.

He pulled his hand away and stood. She fell forward a half step into the space he vacated, barely catching her balance along the edge of the couch. He clenched his hands at his sides to keep from reaching out to steady her. "Apologies." Kit just managed to bite back the stammer of his words, his need to run from the room. "Excuse me."

Kit walked past her, walked around the couch so he was not tempted to sit again at her side, walked to the door and un-locked it, pulled it open, slipped from the room.

It took all of his will not to look back at her as the door closed behind him. He leaned back against the painted wood, not knowing what it was he truly wanted to do. One hand was clenched and pressed against one gold leafed panel, the other remained curled about the handle itching to turn.

What was the matter with him?

What spell were the elves weaving this time?

What if his father chose the blond or the scarlet woman over the girl with the black hair?

It was so much darker than black though. Would it be as soft to the touch as the night sky to a child's dreams? Could he trust it, her, if it was?

Surely the king would recognize the difference between the woman and choose the staid witch over her sisters. Surely he knew his son would feel most kinship with a witch as dour as himself.

The sound that broke from his lips was half sob and half chuckle.

Mayhap it would be easier to bear if his father chose either of the other women over the one the last living part of his soul wanted to betray his memories for.

"**K**it?"

The knocking at his door roused him from the light doze he'd been enjoying in the chair he'd pulled out to his balcony. He stretched slowly, working the kinks from his spine and arms, knowing that his father would not be pleased to be kept waiting while Kit dallied.

He stumbled over to his clothing from the night before, evidence that no servant had come to him yet this day, and the king was here to ring in the new dawn that Kit had hoped to sleep through. He kicked the boots and suit towards his wardrobe, the only effort he was willing to make this early and grabbed the robe slung over the end of his unslept in bed.

He opened the door, knowing better than to try and block his father from entering his rooms though Kit refused entry to the king's guards.

He was no threat to the man. Hells, if the king died, Kit would be stuck ruling a land he desperately hoped would supplant him the moment anyone offered him a throne. For that alone, he'd protect his father with his life, willingly done, even.

"Can I help you, father?" He kept his tone modestly contrite, expecting a tongue lashing over his disappearance the evening before, for not having attended whatever meetings he'd missed this morning.

The king moved through Kit's bedroom, ignoring Kit's question, touching the silks of Kit's unrumpled bed, the curtains that Kit refused to draw closed for fear of the walls closing around him. Ancient fingers glided over the waxed surface of Kit's dining table, the covers of the books and papers strewn over the wood, refuting the main use of the piece of furniture. Leon walked to the balcony and stood staring at the chair set there until Kit joined him in the doorway, waiting.

"I'm tired, boy."

Was he meant to respond to the statement? If so, Kit didn't know how.

"I'm tired of ruling, of these balls, of the endless stream of grievances and petitions that shuffle through my doors daily. I'm tired of looking at my only child and seeing a ghost of the man he once was."

He met his father's gaze as the man sat in Kit's chair.

"When you were a child, I had to set three guards around your room, two at the door and one at the window. No matter how many times I told you of the danger, you still climbed down the trellis and found a way to touch the earth and the trees of our lands. If you'd known how to ride, no doubt you'd've flown all the way to the woods and the demons who wanted you dead within them." He smiled tiredly. "Thank the gods you learned control before taking to the saddle.

"I had the trellis removed once. That didn't stop you from trying to climb down the walls with your tiny hands gripping at tiny cracks between stones. Thankfully your guards were watching you so closely, too afraid to distract you from your task, but ready to catch you should you fall.

"You were never afraid of the fall, Kit. You lived. Even when your mother died, you never wasted a day.

"Then you came back with that woman from the forest, and there was a darkness to you I'd not known before. I saw it in the way you looked at her; knew something she'd done had hurt you to your core and you were fighting your way back to yourself. And you returned, boy, you did. You came back stronger than you'd been. You smiled and talked. There was a lightness to your steps every time she was around. And she was safe, treating you only as her prince, a soldier's job to protect and defend.

"But it wasn't that, was it? She was as charmed by you as you were by her. And I was too blind to see what it meant." He sat forward in the seat, reaching for Kit's hand. When had the king's hand grown so old, lost their strength? Poor man to seek in his son the will he'd long lost. Poor father to find out too late the son was as bad off. Kit clutched the hand holding his, offering what comfort he could, knowing it likely wouldn't matter in the end. "If she'd returned with you, after everything that had happened, would you have come back to me? Would you have found your way from the darkness?"

He answered the only way he could: "The Darkness is all consuming, Father. It takes us all in the end."

His father sat back in the chair, dropped Kit's hand from his grasp, eyes searching Kit's face for what Kit didn't know. "You will never love anyone the way you loved your Captain. You will marry for duty. If I died today, you would rule for the same reason. But you would remain this shell you've become." He stood slowly from the sunken chair. "Is there no way to bring you back?"

"One, but the gods do not return the dead to the living world."

He had not meant to say the words. His father longed as heartily for his lost love as did Kit. It was cruel to remind the man of the same.

"If I could release you from this life, Kit, know that I would."

The king squeezed Kit's shoulder, the motion of a man to another man, not blood to blood, father to son. It must be easier to consider Kit as other than child. Gods knew Kit found it easier to forget that the man he served was also his father.

Knowing that his life counted only for the benefit of the kingdom was not a comforting thought.

It was not precisely true, but he'd not had a childhood like the peasants and courtiers. When he was young… But he'd never really been young.

The old man shuffled to the balustrade, leaned over the hard marble to stare at the patio below. A few couples ranged the walkways to the gardens, some in deeply improper poses when they thought they could not be spied by anyone else. Kit watched the smirk on his father's face, bereft of the condemnation that he expected to see at the display. "The blonde seems most voluptuous, but those damned dresses conceal too much."

Kit joined the king at the rail, settling so that his back was to the gardens, leaning against the stone and tilting his head up to the cloudless sky. Dawn was chilly this morning, and the robe did little to keep the bite of the wind from his flesh.

He did not say anything in response to his father's words.

"The redhead seems spirited, or at the very least she seems to enjoy the dance which will serve her well in our court. She would likely demand you continue to throw balls, son, just to make you waltz." An unhappy thought, though the king had likely meant it as a jest. "Not her though, is it boy? There's only the one who calls to you, and even she you would deny if I allowed it."

Wise man, to know how desperately Kit wished he could.

The king touched his shoulder, and Kit turned in kind, facing the gardens below and the few people who had spotted them from below. Leon waved and Kit followed suit, regal to a fault.

The king stepped back from the rail, into the shade of the palace walls, beyond the sight of the people staring.

Kit didn't care enough to hide, wondered who else might have seen him at his midnight wonderings on the balcony. No one had said aught to him as of yet. "Which one would you choose for me, Father? Which elf shall I take to bride?"

"Give me something, Kit." The hands were stronger now as the pulled at Kit's arm, forced him to face his father and the desperation on the man's face. "I would see you happy in this marriage. I would have it bring you a measure of peace if it might. Which of those women would heal you? Give me something to help you, boy!"

"But I am healed, Father."

"Christophe—"

He pulled away from the man, jerked out of his hold and stared back out over the gardens, deserted now that a repast had been rung, the echoes of the bels still lingering in the air calling those awake to the dining tables.

"Kit…it is not a betrayal to find what joy you can, despite the love you have lost."

No, it wasn't a betrayal. The betrayal came long ago when that love was never taken, and now yearned for another without consideration of it having vanished. "The blond."

"But—"

"You asked my opinion, and I have given it. Do not ask more of me." Kit could not mask the bitterness in his voice, nor did he try to hide the pain in his expression when he turned back to the man and watched his father flinch away.

Give him the light. Keep him from the dark. He would not be reminded of the woman he missed or the devil come to taunt him with the wanting.

"As you wish, son."

Kit did not move as his father left him alone on the balcony. The door to his rooms closed quietly, and he bowed his head, wanting only to escape, not knowing where he would run to.

He wondered how far he could ride before the sun set.

He wondered what he could escape, and what would catch him if he fled.

A last ride, and then he'd accept his fate.

Six

The stable hand yawned at Kit's approach, but managed a tired smile. He handed Kit gloves before walking away to bring Oberon from the stalls.

Kit waited patiently, soothed by the ritual he thwarted as often as embraced. He adjusted the fingers of his left hand, rubbed his palm over his thigh. There was a scuff on his riding boot, not that he cared, but he bent over, scraped at the mark while he waited for the white horse to be saddled and brought to him.

He looked up at the clomping of hooves, the mare and his stallion dancing around each other.

He looked over his shoulder at the woman walking towards him, legs encased in tan breeches, a billowing shirt of black rippling around her with her steps. She wore her full mask, and a hood, hiding what color hair she had beneath it, though he knew by her steady lope it was not his glass slippered lady from last night before but one of her sisters.

The groom left Oberon at Kit's side, brought the mare to the woman and helped her to mount.

Kit said nothing, and she was obviously silent with her spelled voice and would not expect conversation as such.

She nudged her horse forward and he followed.

They moved well together, he accepted her lead as they walked slowly through the city. She stopped in the square, her face moving to the buildings and the shops, the merchants just beginning to bring their wares to their stalls for the day. Her head paused while turned to the baker, Cinta's fresh cinnamon and ground clove rolls filling the air as the man left his shop to lay a tray of fresh pastries on his table. Kit found his eyes drawn to the delicacies as well, nudged his horse over and smiled at the man, the grateful stare in return for a life saved so long ago.

He requested two of the treats, which the baker supplied readily enough, waving off Kit's offered coin in exchange. Kit smiled for the male, and insisted on the payment.

She watched him return to her side, her mare sidling beside Oberon while Kit handed her the cinnamon roll to eat.

He watched the way her hand lifted delicately to remove a small panel over her lips, the mask still held in place to shield her.

Red lips like berries growing on the vines in the groves of the palace.

He rode with the sun-kissed lady, his offered choice of an hour earlier.

She nodded, and he thought that it was with more understanding than thanks or recognition. Perhaps it was a trait of the elves to pick at their partner's thoughts. He had the impression that she rolled her eyes at him, the quick turn and shake of her head all he had to read her by. But she didn't deny his thoughts, and he sat his horse without condemnation, absurdly content that she might know his mind, and not expect aught else from him because of it.

Once more they kicked their horses into an easy walk, reaching the walls of the city and the path beyond. She kept her mare to an easy trot, and he followed her lead, wondering where she would take him if he said nothing to gainsay her. They turned towards the wooded path. Branches soon obscured the sun, forming an arch over their heads as they passed onto the forest road.

Beyond sight of the city watch, beneath the dark trees of her homeland, she removed the hood over her head, pulled the pins holding her braid to her crown so that the long yellow tail flowed down her back. She swayed on her mount, moving naturally with the horse's rhythm, her hair following the motion. The braid swinging like a pendulum, entrancing him, stealing his focus. To think that so simple a thing could hypnotize him. Yet even knowing he was being drawn into her spell, he did nothing to stop it. He would see what she wished him to see, and would not fight her.

They moved from the path into the woods. He recognized the trees only so much as to say that they could have been the same trees he'd ridden through the month prior in search of a ghost deep in the depths. Her mount wove smoothly through the thickets, and his followed without pause.

He leaned back in his seat, ignoring the discomfort of the saddle to lay prone on the horse's back, stare at the thick leaves above him.

One said green blade drifted down from the canopy on a light breeze.

Kit opened his hand, reaching up to catch the delicate leaf. Even here in the twilight of the woods, there were so many colors of green in one single shaft of life. Whirls of yellow, lines of forest pine, veins of something closer to black, and all so bright in the darkness. He watched the way the branches swayed and listened to the whispering of waving foliage. No wonder the elves found such sanctuary beneath the trees.

His horse stopped, and Kit drew himself back into his seat.

She held his horse's reins, dropped when he reclined along the beast. He hadn't heard her dismount, but now she stared up at him from the depths of her mask, and he waited for whatever she would have of him. She led the stallion further down the path, walking at his side while he rode. Where they passed, it was like only he left an imprint on the world, her presence one with the wood around them.

He ducked beneath a low hanging branch and beyond was a wide circle surrounding a central tree. He felt a vague sense of recognition, of panic, but it passed soon enough, or perhaps his apathy just held sway within his breast.

The rustling around him drew his gaze to the canopy, his eyes taking in the homes built within the giant trees, rope bridges connecting them to each other, the men and women lining the walks and staring as intently down at him as he stared up at them. He could not tell their expressions, too far away to make out smiles or frowns, what their whispered words might be saying about him. They didn't matter, in the end, when the Priestosolos emerged from the great tree in the center of the clearing, and even the wind stopped whistling through the wood at her approach.

She stopped on the last step to her tree, her hands spread wide, head tilted to the boughs and the people there. "Blood has been spilled, and blood has been paid." Surely if she had told them of his attack, he would not be so easily allowed entrance into their homeland? But he could see the mark of his knife still fresh upon her throat, and wondered if her people knew the true meaning behind it. "The Darkness demands that any who make the sacrifice be admitted to our grove if they seek our shelter. Are there any among you who would gainsay this man the right to be here?"

"*Qui forsome slobec mistaf?*" What offering has been made?

Kit could not see the speaker, nor tell if the voice was male or female. He stiffened at the challenge of the tone, could guess well enough their meaning. Asked the same question himself, though remained silent, unwilling, even in his suicidal thoughts, to condemn himself.

The priestess motioned and his guide raised her hand in support to help him dismount. His hesitation was not remarked upon, and her hand did not waver, but it took him longer to meet whatever fate awaited him than he thought it would. Now that the time had come he was afraid.

His boots thumped into the carpet of grass, bending the delicate blades beneath his tread. A breath of wind swept before him, creating a path to the center of the glade and he did not need his guide's hand to tell him to follow where the breeze led him. He found it easier to look at the priest as he moved, and she held his stare until he was before her.

A second gold masked woman appeared at his other side, her presence making itself known out of the corner of his eye.

They caged him, and he wondered if the black haired elf was at his back waiting to catch him if he turned to run.

"Kneel, Prince."

No, he did not think he—but hands grabbed at his arms and pushed him to the ground. His knees struck the earth harder than he thought they meant for him to fall, but their grips did not loosen about him. They held him tighter, and he did not fight when they pulled his arms roughly behind his back to hold him still.

The priestess drew a knife from beneath the sleeves of her robes. The garment flowed with her as she descended the stair and crossed the distance to where he waited. She stood before him and pressed the point of the knife beneath his chin, the tip just grazing the node of his Adam's apple.

He met her gaze for a moment, seeing the same aloof disinterest he felt swirling in his own blood. With a small smile, he tipped his head back, eyes closed as he waited to feel the knife pierce him.

The tear of cloth parted by the knife jerked him away from visions of his death, enough that he struggled to understand what was happening and did not fight the women who stripped his shirt from his shoulders, bared his scars to this world of elf and Night. They caught him quickly enough when he flinched and tried to draw away, pulling at his arms to restrain him, knees pressed tight to his back so he was forced to bend awkwardly and rely on them for his balance, his shame bare for all those who wished him dead to see.

"Blood has been spilled so that ours would not. Blood has been paid and is honored. Will anyone speak against him?"

What in the gods' names was going on?

Around him the whispering of the wind, the gentle melody of tinkling leaf fall and feathering grass stilled. No voice was raised in question or protest and he did not know what to do.

She bent towards him, her eyes holding his, concerned, if he had to guess, though why she should care he didn't know. "You came expecting to die. You do not carry a sword or shield. You walk calmly into our ranks and would give your life without struggle," she tilted her head and it was far too similar to Eli for his comfort or his sanity. "Why, Prince?"

His lips parted in a grim parody of a smile, one that did not try to hide the ache he harbored within. "The struggle is to live, my lady. Death seems a relief." His whispered words did not move beyond her hearing, but they still seemed too loud to his ears. He could not regret the speaking of his darkest secret, not here where the Darkness knew all things.

She reached and took his chin in her hand, the knife in her other still held threateningly enough. The warmth of her flesh surprised him, though he didn't know why. He thought she would be as cold as he was, but she was flesh and blood and life. She looked over his shoulder and he watched her nod.

The silence reigned.

The knees against his back fell away, allowed the exaggerated arc of his spine to relax. He found it did nothing to relieve the unsteady beating of his heart nor the rasp of his breath before his enemies.

"Not enemies. Enemies no more."

He did not trust his voice to gainsay her, not that he thought she would allow the words with her power.

She lifted her knife once more, and he closed his eyes, unwilling to watch. If the blade made a sound he did not hear it as it sliced into skin. There was no pain though the scent of iron filled the air between them and he wondered at the lack of feeling to his wound.

He blinked, and she handed the blade to the woman on his left. A bead of blood welled on the pad of her thumb, staining her pale flesh red.

She knelt before him and his heartbeat sped faster and he stared at the darkness swirling in her eyes.

With tender slowness, she pressed the drop of blood to the skin over his heart.

"For the Iisforsos. You are accepted among us."

His head tilted, eyes widening at the gesture, not knowing the name.

She walked around him, and he turned as much as he was able with his guardians holding him, to follow her movements.

He needn't have strained, for he tensed when her hands settled against his bare shoulders from behind to hold him in place.

His fingers clenched and unclenched, and then it began.

Elf after elf stepped forward, the rustling in the branches signally their descent to the earth to reach him. Each blooded their finger on the knife in his guide's hand, each pressed a mark across his chest. Each accepted him for the Iisforsos and he wondered that he did not know this name they committed him to.

He watched as best he could the lines they formed across his skin in blood. Along his collarbones, down his sternum, tracing over his ribs, dipping along the bones of his hips and pelvis. Each touch made words gather along his tongue, brought him closer to the edge of asking why, what was the point, when would he die, but his lips remained sealed, and he knelt receiving the bloody tribute bestowed upon him.

And finally relaxed into whatever inevitability awaited him.

It took a lifetime, and it took no time at all. Old faces and young, men and women, children and grandparents, they all came and they all marked him. His arms were released, and bloody prints pressed over his biceps, traced his fingers. She hummed behind him, and he realized that her tune held him captive, was as part of the spell her people were weaving as the blood they painted him with.

The elves did not return to their homes after touching him. Far worse, they gathered around him, their presence sometimes ten deep in spaces as they waited and watched him and his chance of escape diminished with every body that closed in the space until only a single alley remained for those left to walk through and press their blood to his skin.

"Ashasolos." High Servant of the Forge.

The male stepped forward, arms heavily muscled from hard labor, face burned from the sun, and yet with a peace to his countenance that Kit envied for this was a man content with himself. He stepped forward, and knelt as the priestess had knelt, pierced his thumb as the woman had pierced hers, braced a hand on Kit's shoulder, and placed a blood print to Kit's forehead. The man smiled at the mark, his hands covering the woman's at Kit's neck, and leaned forward, pressing his lips to Kit's though there was nothing sexual about the embrace, soothing, compassionate instead.

"For Iis, you are welcomed by Ashet."

The man stood and took his place at the front of the wall of souls surrounding Kit.

"Chimsolos." Earth's Venerated Lady.

The woman who stepped from the crowd had once approached Kit already, the first time with a young child in her arms. The infant had wailed at the pricking of a finger, but calmed upon touching Kit's skin, the gentle soothing cluck of the lady's tongue.

He had not noticed that the Nurturer had not made her own mark against his flesh.

Now the woman knelt as her brother had a moment before, pierced her finger and drew a line from his lower lip to the tip of his chin. Her lips were soft where the man's had been strong. She kissed him with as little passion, and yet as much heady acceptance.

"For Iis, you are welcomed by Rouchim."

Kit touched his tongue to the wetness when she stood away, tasted iron in his mouth but did not flinch from the tang.

"Elichisolos." Master of the Final Midnight.

He tensed as the assassin stepped from the crowd.

The man was shorter than Eli had been.

Kit had hoped—

For a moment Kit had hoped that all of this was just a ritual; that at the end of everything, she would be the one to walk from the crowd and mark him as her own. How foolish of him to pray for something he knew would not occur. He closed his eyes, not wanting to look at this man who had, in all likelihood, been tasked with taking his predecessor's life.

The male pressed his thumb to Kit's temple and dragged his finger across Kit's closed lids from one side of his face to the other.

This kiss held none of the heart or warmth of the others, but neither did it bestow aggression. It was, and so Kit accepted it, knowing that the touch, granted in such a way, was significant as it did not foretell his death for a moment longer. Kit blinked his eyes opened, stared into the face that was so familiar to him and alien at the same time. The eyes, the assassin had Eli's eyes, and Kit jerked away at the meeting of his lost love's father.

"For Iis, you are welcomed by Echi."

Kit shuddered at the benediction, and though the tone was static, the words themselves were filled with acceptance.

The high priestess released Kit's shoulders and it took him a moment to realize that he was no longer held by the women who brought him to this place. He remained rooted to the ground, though he watched the Pristosolos as she knelt once more before him.

"Lieasolos." The Healer.

She raised the knife again, but instead of her thumb, this time she pierced her palm, letting the blood well in her cupped hand. When the red made a small pool against her flesh, she handed the knife to her Daughter at his side, and met his gaze once more. She gripped his shoulder, leaned into his body, and placed her palm over the first mark she'd made against his chest.

A high wind whipped through the trees overhead, leaves fluttering to the ground in the gale.

She did not look away, and he found himself unable to, pelted with the soft green hail.

When the storm quieted, when the silence reigned once more, she leaned forward and kissed his blooded lips.

"For Iis, you are welcomed by Liaea." This she said to him and to the crowd around them, gathered to witness this moment, which he still did not understand and was unsure that he desired the knowledge. "You are one of us now. You are worthy of her, though perhaps it was we who had to prove we were worthy of you as well." The High Priestess, the High Healer, smiled gently at him, bent forward and kissed his brow.

She stood and he looked up at her from his place on his knees. "Marked by blood, bound by blood, we welcome our brother to the woods."

He flinched at the sudden cacophony around him, men and women cheering as he was helped to his feet and the priestess took his hands in hers, a final kiss to each of his scarred palms.

Her fingers lingered over the ring, and her eye caught his, and he wondered what it was she saw in his gaze, what the odd gleam in hers meant.

She leaned close, careful not to smear the still wet marks on his skin though the breeze had done much in drying the blood covering him. "She is waiting for you at your ball, fair prince. Go to her, and find the peace you're looking for."

Go to her...

Yes, he would go to the woman he was fated now to marry. Accepted into the fold because he was to be bound to one of their own. Forgiven the blood debt against him because his father had signed a godsdamned peace treaty with these elves and his was the flesh that would fulfill the promise of that contract. Accepted for he had paid dearly for that debt and would remember the marks on his skin for his life.

He wanted to rage. He wanted to snarl.

How dare she mark him! How dare she not take his life!

He'd come fully expecting, fully prepared to die. That he was being denied by yet another party infuriated him. That he was being bound by another party to a fate beyond his choosing broke him. He had counted on the Dienobolos refusing to part with one of their Daughters in marriage to a city dweller. He had counted on the fast tempers and tempered cruelty to end him before the day came where he took one of theirs again as his own.

They failed him.

Gentle hands turned him away from the Mother Tree, turned him towards his horse and his exit from this accursed grove.

His fists clenched, wanting to lash out, strike, destroy. He was 'of the forest' now; if he killed one of these people, they would be bound to kill him in turn.

Just one. Just kill one of them and he would be free.

And yet the faces surrounding him smiled, and some smiled with a hint of sadness in their eyes, some with joy, most with a wary mix of acceptance and trepidation, but no pity. They'd been the ones to see him broken when he first emerged from the tower. They'd known the worst of what was done to him. But they didn't pity him, and he didn't see hate in their stares.

His fingers unclenched. His eyes closed and he let himself be led away.

His shirt was in tatters, but it was all he had and the hands leading him helped him into the ruined linen. Oberon was led to him, and he climbed blindly up into the saddle, eyes unfocused as he gave the horse its head.

"Wash the blood away, Prince. Your people would not understand our ritual, and the sign will not need to be read by my Daughter for her to know you've been accepted."

He turned in his saddle to look at the woman standing before the open doorway to the tree temple. His horse moved restlessly beneath him, and Kit nodded once, not knowing how to respond, before leaving the forest far behind him.

The woods thinned into distinctive paths. He didn't bother to direct his mount, the animal seemingly knowing which road to take to return to the city.

For a time, Oberon followed a stream, the merry trickling of the water grated on Kit's nerves, but he stopped, as he had been commanded, and dismounted. He stripped his shirt from his shoulders. Dried flakes of blood drifted from his skin and settled in the trickling water. He watched as the red washed away in the current, knelt, and lifted handfuls of the sun warmed water to his chest, his face. He used a rock rubbed smooth beneath the stream to rinse the red smears from him. Kit dunked his whole head in the cold, clearing the fog from his mind, returning to his unwanted reality.

He washed his skin until his distorted reflection ran clear in the water.

The midday sun dried his flesh quickly enough.

He dressed and mounted and found his way back to the road and the city beyond, exhaustion weighing heavily upon him as he left his horse with the grooms and made his way to his chambers. No one stopped him, no one seemed to wonder at his absence or question his dazed look.

At the stroke of midnight, she would stand before him and he would take the mask from her face. He would have a bride, and she would have for a husband a broken man lost to memories of a love he'd never truly known.

He wished the elves had killed him

He wept that they had not.

H e woke to the shuffling creep of his valet trying to be silent while preparing Kit's clothing for the evening. The poor man flinched when Kit sat up in the bed, but said nothing, not even to direct Kit to the bathroom where the tub was already filled with steaming water, bergamot soap waiting on the cloth at the side. He shut the door so that he would have privacy while he bathed and so that he could undress without prying eyes. Even his servants still sought to sneak glances of him, their eyes misting over when they saw his scars. He was more worried that they might see specks of dried blood coloring his flesh than anything else.

He stripped and stared at himself in the long mirror against the wall of the room. Nothing different about him that he could see, nothing to denote his woodland adventures, no mark to call the elf to him. At least he had some muscle tone back. His ribs were still pronounced but not so much as to be obscene. Dark bruises colored the skin beneath his eyes, but he'd always looked tired, or so his father told him. His hair hadn't grown past his ears, but the barbers kept it well shaped. Besides the multitude of scars covering him, he looked like any other poor soldier. Only he bathed in a pool with scented oils and dressed in velvets and satins and had someone else polish his boots every morning.

His hands clenched, short nails biting into his palms. Yes, he could feel the pressure, might even consider it pain, but it was dulled. He could feel her tracing symbols against his palm, but most of what he felt came from memories of what he'd grabbed or scratched or rubbed before.

Kit climbed into the tub, sitting back in the marble bath so that only his head was above the water resting on a folded towel left for that purpose. He stared at the ceiling, the painting of Atha cradling an infant in her arms. The infant had Kit's face, and the goddess looked like his mother, or at least that's what he'd been told when he asked after the models.

He sat in the small pool until the sun touched the horizon and the water turned cold to the touch.

Dried, a towel wrapped around his waist, he unlocked the door and moved towards his bed, the candles adding light to the quickly fading sun beyond his windows.

"Your father requested it, sire."

Kit touched the green brocade on his bed, gold leaves sewn onto the fabric with the closures buttoned down his chest. How appropriate.

"It's fine."

The man tarried, unsure whether to offer assistance or leave as was Kit's usual preference.

Honestly, Kit didn't know what he wanted either.

"How long till the bells ring to signal the start of the ball?"

"Two hours, sire."

He let the towel drop to the floor and picked at the undergarments laid beside his attire for the night. "Find me in two hours then."

"Yes, m'lord."

Kit pulled the small clothes over his legs, breeches, shirt and boots. The jacket he slung over his arm, unwilling to put the coat on before he had to. The moment the velvet covered him, he would have no choice but to acknowledge what would happen when the clock struck the darkest hour.

His guards came to attention, readying to form ranks around him. "I'm heading to the barracks."

He did not tell them why, and they did not ask, but at least they knew well enough not to follow him down the side stairs and across the way to the training yard. The soldiers there stopped to nod at him, looking to one another to see why he was upon the sands. When he ignored them, they returned to their drills, though he felt their gaze lingering on his back as he went to Eli's rooms and let himself through the door. Carefully, he closed the panel behind him, pushed the lock into place, hung his coat on a hook in the closet and closed that door too before he turned back to the room and its greenery.

It took him less than ten minutes.

It took Kit less than ten minutes to smash every vase, every pot, cover the flooring in thick dirt, broken leaves, torn roots so destroyed they could not be transplanted, never be saved. He flung the chairs against the walls, shattering the legs into broken timber. The vine canopy he yanked and pulled till it fluttered in tatters from its rails. He trampled dirt onto the bedspread, used his knife to cut the mattress and pillows and pull the white feather stuffing out to mix with the destruction on the ground.

Ten minutes, and what was left of her presence was destroyed and nothing felt soothed in his soul.

He'd not broken the windows. The bathroom remained intact. Opening her wardrobe had seemed too personal, and he didn't want to touch her clothing, see his shirts that had found their way into her closet, her scent mingling with his.

He fell to his knees in the dirt, his hands curled together, fingers stroking the brown that coated him, and sobbed.

Kit sobbed and it went against everything a man should be, should ever do.

And he didn't give a rat's ass.

The door opened and closed slowly. No more thumping of swords or clanging of steel outside the small space. Poor fool, whoever had been sent to see what commotion he was causing.

But it wasn't a male's tread that crossed over the broken pots and shards of ceramic to come to his side. Her hand settled against the back of his neck and he wondered how she'd managed to find him, and why she'd been the one to come looking.

He did not struggle when she led him to stand and walked with him to the bathing chambers. Her hands pushed him against the cream painted stucco beside the wash sink. She took his dirt smudged fingers in her own, her black gloves such a contrast against his flesh. Her head shook and he had the impression that she was looking at his face from behind her mask, but he could not see her eyes with the gauze covering them.

No, that wasn't true. He could see the moon white skin of her face, but her eyes themselves were pools of black, no white within them, no iris he could discern. Blind, he thought, but she touched him with such surety that she had to have her sight. The dark pools of her eyes were as black as her hair, blacker, if he had to guess.

She did not stop him when he cupped her masked cheek in his stained palm. "So beautiful, your Darkness."

The gold was smooth beneath his touch as she turned her head, pressed the fake lips to his skin in an imitation of a kiss.

She stopped only to pull her gloves off before taking his hands once more, turning the faucet so that the water warmed and she could wash the dirt from his flesh. He caught her when she tried to pull away, but she looked at him with those void-dark eyes and he let her go only so far as the small cabinet against the opposite wall, pulling out a cloth and returning to the running water, dampening the cotton before reaching to wash the dirt from his face and neck. Her fingers opened the ties of his shirt, trailed over his skin while he leaned his head back, allowing her access to whatever she wished to touch.

With a gentleness born of a healer's touch, she stripped his shirt from him.

He watched those midnight eyes as she looked over his chest, her fingers passing a breath above his scars.

She trembled, and he realized she shed silent tears for him.

"Did you not look your fill that day in the woods?"

Her face tipped up to his. Her eyes widened at his understanding.

He should hate her for taking Eli's face, for making him dream for even a moment that he was with the woman he lost. But he had nothing in him with which to care, and his father's choice of wife would not matter as she was the only one left to have.

Her hands shook, but she turned back to her task and stroked the cloth over his skin. A droplet ran from his collarbone down his chest. She pressed her hand to his flesh, her bare hand to his stomach, her calluses and scars pressing against his, stopping the drop from falling any further down his torso.

There was a different sort of tremble to her limbs now, an answering quake in his own body that wanted to respond.

She met his gaze when he reached to touch her hair, curl the black silken strands between his fingers, step closer into her body, the towel forgotten between them.

A knock sounded beyond the small room at the door to the apartments.

Instinct had him pushing her behind him, using his body as her shield though the door was locked and no one tried to force their way into the room.

It took two swallows before his voice was steady enough to respond with a gruff "What?" The terse word was the best he could manage.

"You said to find you at the bells, my lord. They are about to start ringing and I—"

Kit heard the hesitation in the young voice.

His valet broke the spell her soft touch had woven over him.

That she thought to magic him into having feelings for her made his head hurt with anger and the longing made that anger burn all the brighter.

He was afraid. He was afraid that it was not her magic that wrapped him in desire, but some small spark of life that remained and desired to thrive in her presence.

She tugged his arm, turned him back to her and it was all he could do to maintain the anger in his thoughts, the sneer on his face.

He would not be swayed by the tears gathering in her black eyes.

She tried to push him back against the wall, but he would not budge. The spell binding her voice prevented her from even uttering a sound of displeasure, for which he was grateful, not having wanted to hear her tears or her frustration. That didn't stop her though, the hand she pressed once more to his bare chest slapping against his skin, succeeding in pushing him away from her for a moment in time.

He growled; bared his teeth like some feral animal that hunted the woods. Maybe she would understand his threat better if he emulated some kin of hers, wild, untamed.

Or not, since she stepped closer and he met the unanswered response in her gaze.

How he used to love inciting a similar reaction in her once-sister. Watching Eli react to some brazen remark had been one of the greatest highlights of his day.

She shook her head, so similar to his Captain, that he felt the ache more keenly. Now he felt her magic, a distinct thing from what feelings had woven around them a minute before. Her magic surrounded him, pulled cloth from the darkness and wrapped him in its embrace. The softest of silks fit tailor made to his skin. He could feel the heat of her hand through the shirt she dressed him in, pristine by her grace.

When she drew her hand back, he longed. He longed for the heat of her to return.

This time he went when she pulled him, retreating over the dirt strewn floors that slowly cleaned as he passed, broken pots reforming, soil lifting in the air to fill them, leaves ripped apart reknit and found their homes in their vases once more. Even the canopy over the bed reformed, though the wispy strands with flowers on them were left where they fell, like some artful seduction which the destruction had revealed. Feathers floated back into the bedding and ripped cloth received neat, invisible stitches to put them back together.

Did she expect gratitude for repairing what his sorrow had broken?

To be sure, the apology for the mess stuck in his throat.

He stopped before the door, his mouth open to speak what words he didn't know. She pressed her fingers to his lips, stilled his apology, his gratitude.

The elf stepped against the wall, out of sight of the door and the servant standing sentinel outside.

Kit pulled his jacket from the closet, finally tearing his gaze from hers though he felt her watching his every move. He made to sling the coat on, but her hands stopped him once more, helped him once more, smoothing his shoulders, resettling the closures at his throat and down his chest. She leaned into him, and he rested his chin atop her head, his arms wrapped around her waist to keep her close.

The valet knocked again, and Kit disentangled himself gently from his elf. He cupped her gold covered cheeks, stared into the dark pools of her eyes, and turned back to the door. He did not look back in his exit.

Eight

K it left her there with a flourish, snapping his fingers to hurry his poor valet along, allow her a chance to leave without witnesses to her presence. It was one thing for a man, even a prince, to sweep a woman away, but another entirely for a woman to approach a man.

He was used to it, used to having to protect his companion when they did not realize the danger themselves. Eli had never cared what others thought of her actions. It must be an elf mentality.

His valet pulled him to a stop outside the ballroom, grumbling about dirt stains and scuffed shoes and how had Kit managed it all in the space of two hours. Kit was almost amused by the endless chatter, the harangue, distracted from the ball by this young boy and the dark elf.

Unfortunately, the distraction did not last nearly long enough, and Kit remembered why tonight was both relief and devastation all too soon.

Today was in truth the day of his birth. The fanfare for his introduction would be the grandest of the three days. All those who had gathered for this final night would sink low in curtsies and bows and he would walk down the center of the aisle they made for him and take his seat on his father's throne. Leon would absent himself, as it was Kit's right to rule someday, so let him feel the weight of said power on a less grandiose scale.

But beyond the introductions, this was the least formal night of them all. For once Kit took his seat, and with his father gone, no one held to the strict dictates of society for Kit himself would have it so.

Most of the attendees had formed their clicks and had established partners for dances well in advance of the musicians striking up the first notes of whatever song they chose to perform. Everyone had their partners, and Kit smiled at the ladies designated to beg him for a dance, though usually he was allowed to rest, not expected to take every hand offered to him on this last of days.

He wondered how this year would be different, at what point his father would appear and make the announcement that everyone had waited for for centuries: that Kit had found a wife, and one of the dancers would someday be queen.

There had been a time, in the early years, when Kit was young and he pretended that there was a chance of him choosing someone he loved, that Kit would stumble upon his father in the midst of a rehearsal, standing with a mug or whatever he was drinking before an empty room rousing the ghosts of his court to cheers at Kit's bride. More often than not, Eli had been with Kit for the performance, and they had sat in the library long after the king had left listing off the qualities that seemed most important for a prince's bride. Everything from the ability to call birds to her side with the notes of a song, to being able to spin straw out of gold, or was it straw into gold? It was more amusing still to leave the invented lists on the king's desk or somewhere where a courtier might see it and the ensuing panic it would cause. Leon would stomp red faced through the palace. And inevitably a woman would attend the year later with a live bird leashed to her gown or a ball of thread dyed the crispest of golds. The woman with the thread had tried to tether Kit with it. Eli had disavowed the tradition after that. Leon too had kept his musings silent in the aftermath.

Kit shook his head, clearing the memories from before his eyes. Gods, but why didn't the thought hurt as much as before? He did not want to let go of the pain.

Trumpets sounded. The nattering of the ballroom grew quiet and footmen pushed the doors open. His valet stepped aside and Kit stepped forward.

He kept his hands at the small of his back and walked with his eyes trained on the noble steed above the throne. He walked up the stairs to the dais, turned and watched the ranks of men and women sink low in their formal attire to honor their prince, a man they likely knew very little about beyond rumors and gossip. They rose, and he bowed in return, gratitude for their obeisance. He rose, and the musicians went into a lively quadrille. He sat on the throne, and watched the colors of the various ball gowns swirl around him.

Ignobis was absent, his brides with him. No black dressed Daughters of the Dienobolos waited in the throngs of people to steal a final dance. His father had not sought him out to tell Kit which bride would step through the doors at midnight. Kit wouldn't tell the older man that the elves had decided without input from the king.

Kit stared at the doors through which he'd entered, stared unseeing at the gilded arches, hands loosely clenched on the arms of his chair. The room blurred with memory, with wishes.

The third night of the ball.

She'd walked in late, as she had every evening prior. Her gown was black, and yet beautiful in its austerity. The dress had been fitted beneath her breasts, the creamy swells of her flesh much too prominent for the fashion of his people, but she hadn't cared. A single emerald stone had sat in the hollow of her throat, bringing color to her auburn hair and bright green eyes. There had been mischief around her, and when she'd moved, and her dress had revealed the shape of her legs behind the fabric, the courtiers had flinched back in horror and he'd been fascinated by the strength of self it would take to ignore all the looks and whispers that surrounded her entrance. She'd worn the same dress all three nights. All three nights, she somehow looked more elegant than the last.

Kit smiled at the woman bowing before his father's throne. She trembled and he wondered how long he'd kept her waiting for him to notice her. So Kit stood in recompense and extended his hand, led the young girl into the reel, even managed to smile at her timid attempt at conversation with him.

She had been silent the first night of the dance, weaving among the patrons without pause, searching. He had wondered what it was she was looking for, had had to ask. When he stopped before her, she had run into him, not even knowing he was there, perhaps knowing but who could say. "Would you dance with me?" And she hadn't refused.

Her fingers had been cold in his, and he'd taken a tighter grip on her hand, not to hold her to him, but to share his warmth. It was the first time her head had tilted to the side and he had smiled for her. He slipped her arm into his, led her from the dance floor to the table and the champagne waiting.

The glasses were not his intent, and he pulled her to the chairs set along the far wall, held her hands in his, rubbing them gently until they warmed in his grip. "There's nothing to be worried about here, no nerves to give in to." He had stroked her thumb with his, "It's just a dance, my lady."

"Is it not far more than that, my prince?"

"Not tonight."

He accepted the glass of wine thrust into his hand by an overzealous father flouting the virtues of his daughter in the red dress. Yes, of course she was well mannered and had all the courtly graces, dancing, embroidery, song. Kit refrained from asking if the woman knew how to wield a sword or had ever travelled the wild paths of the forest.

Wouldn't it be nice to breathe in the fresh scent of flowers in the garden?

So Kit had obliged and extended his arm and escorted the young woman to the gardens. He doubted there were assassins waiting in the hedgerow, but the girl never looked at the greenery or the roses fighting for an early bloom in this false spring. Her eyes remained on his face, and Kit fought hard to ignore the sycophantic light in her eyes.

He watched her staring at the blackened gardens beyond the lit torches of the patio. The snow had melted during the course of the afternoon but had left the paths muddied and no one dared the pebbled roads to explore the plants just waking from their winter hibernation. "They are lovely in the spring."

She looked quickly at him from the corner of her eye, never fully taking her gaze from what shadow hid behind the glass. "They are so manicured. What of nature remains to them?"

"I have never thought of it before."

"You city folk, ever fearing the untamed trees. Do the deer run freely through the woods have you ever found a shadowed path to linger among?"

"No, my lady, but I have no guide to show me the way."

She smiled and turned her face away, and he wondered if he should ask her if she would be willing to serve such a purpose the next day. A minuet was struck by the orchestra, and Kit looked once more for her hand in the dance. The moment of hesitation which had threatened the night before was gone, and she accepted his touch, her hands warmer today though still cool. "We shall have to find you a glass of brandy."

"Whatever for?"

"To warm you."

"There are other ways to do the same." And her eyes had glinted at him with mischief and he had followed her onto the dance floor, no longer leading but being led.

Three sets he dedicated to her, always coming back throughout the night. Her cheeks grew pink and the green of her eyes darkened with something more than just pleasure in the dance and he wondered what she would say if he asked her to stay.

Kit begged a moment to himself, laughing as he stumbled up the steps, perhaps too many sips of champagne himself this night. Were not men meant to go to their marriages drunk? Not noble men, of a surety.

He was not nearly drunk enough, regardless, and even as he leaned his head back against the throne, the room shifted into focus and steadied about him, waiting.

The gilded clock at the top of the staircase struck the final bell of midnight.

The musicians stood from their seats to riotous applause and Kit turned with his Ella to the performers, raising his glass in salute, letting her hand go so that she might clap as well.

It took him a moment to realize that she was not clapping at his side, that the brief touch of her fingers to his cheek had not been in accidental play but in barest farewell. He turned enough so that he could watch her pushing through the crowd and to the servants' entrance. A white clad maid nearly fell in her haste to make way for the lady rushing past.

Kit blinked, blinked again, and then did not hesitate to follow rushing to reach her retreating form.

The crowd made room for him, hustling to get out of the barreling way of their prince, many unsure of what the emergency was but unwilling to risk facing the expression on Kit's face if they waylaid him.

He reached the courtyard of the palace in time to see her rushing across the grand circular drive to the waiting carriages, no, horses stabled in the yard. She stumbled once and he called for her to stop, resuming his chase as she kicked off her shoe and reached the stallions in the paddock.

Her horse reared when he grabbed the reins but she held her seat. Kit did not deny that he was impressed with her skill even as he fell away and she set her heels to the horse's flanks and through the palace gates.

Surely she knew he would follow?

He blinked the room back into focus, back into the present and the silence that had fallen in the grand space. Nearly as one, the nobles and courtiers had turned to face the staircase and for a moment he was frightened to look up and see which woman stood at its peak.

The gold of her mask had been replaced with a white lace that concealed nothing of her identity even as it hid her from the rest of the crowd, wrapped her in a veil he was privy to see beyond. Her black tresses hung freely about her shoulders, diamond shards woven into the strands, catching the light from the thousands of candles in the chandeliers. There were no straps to her dress, her shoulders bared for the first time since her entrance to the ball. The white of her gown was only a few shades paler than her skin, the faint blush lending a rosy glow to her moonlit flesh. And the gown itself, beyond its striking color, the way it sparkled as though woven with crystals, was unlike anything anyone had worn before. The bodice lifted her breasts while maintaining the slim lines of her figure. Pearls and jewels formed the neckline, emphasized the gentle curve of material over her bosom, highlighted the gold chain that stroked her throat with a lover's caress before slipping into the delicate amount of cleavage she revealed. The skirt, from where it billowed out below her sternum in soft waves of nearly sheer white, shifted and moved with her every breath, settling like a cloud on the ground, waiting only for a wind to blow her away. If she danced, when she danced, her partner would fall into the dream with her.

She looked a ghost, standing in the middle of the hall.

She looked a princess awaiting her prince.

Her hand trembled as she reached for the rail and walked slowly down the stairs to the dance floor. A breath was inhaled and Kit could not tell if it was his alone or if the watchers breathed with him. She stepped onto the dance floor, and a hundred eyes watched her walk the same path he had walked before to meet him at the throne.

It was self-preservation that kept him seated. His legs would have shaken; he might well have fallen on his knees, ready to worship at this woman in white's feet, the silent flash of light before the darkness claimed a soul, the peace that led the spirit into the night.

A clock chimed somewhere within the silent palace. That it was heard was testament to the shock of the people gathered within the ballroom.

The great bells in the tower began to ring.

He counted one and stood. At the second he moved down the steps of the dais and stood upon the wooden floor at the third strike. His stride was measured, not long, not fast, just a pretty dance to be performed for the gathered assemblage as he moved to meet her in the center of the floor, each having crossed the space in silence. She slipped into a shallow curtsy at the fifth toll. Kit bowed for the sixth.

His hand rose and she dipped her head in demure acceptance as he settled her comfortably in his arms for the waltz. The first strains of the violin were hesitant, unwilling to break the spell even as they gained confidence and the prince and his princess danced across the hall.

He spun her to the peal of a bass bell, having lost count of what number tolled.

The orchestra let the last chord of the song ring throughout the hall, broken only by the final tenor chime far overhead.

He pulled her into his chest, buried his face in her hair. She leaned against him and her tears wet the lace of her mask, shattered against the green of his jacket.

"Eli—" He raised his hands to cup her cheeks, look at her beloved face and the changes wrought within it: the hair that was no longer a mix of mahoganies and scarlet, the eyes without their ring of green. He wiped wet drops from her cheeks, not removing the mask from her, allowing her a moment more of her secrets. "I don't understand."

She trembled in his arms. Her hands gripped his shoulders, staring at his throat rather than meeting his gaze, a first for her, for him, he was certain.

"I don't understand."

Chapter IV

She slipped from his arms, fled the question in his gaze, the hope and the despair that she'd put there and that he'd endured because she had not been at his side.

With a knowledge born of centuries of living within these walls, she slipped from the ballroom and down the steps of the palace and into the night beyond.

He would follow her. He always followed her. And when he caught her, she would cry and she would plead because for three days she'd been locked in silence and watched him suffer and she did not know of any way to relieve the pain she'd caused him. Her heart beat with that pain. Her soul ached at the sorrow that bled from his pores.

She ran, stumbling when her slipper caught in the grass and she gasped as her grace deserted her and she watched the ground come reaching up to catch her.

Strong hands closed around her waist, pulled her into a body that wrapped around her and took the brunt of her fall. She landed at his side, spared the harsh impact by his chivalry while he fought to catch his breath beside her. She reached without thought, the darkness that flowed through her veins coming easily to her command, spearing into his body and banishing the pain of a bashed elbow and bruised spine. His back arced beneath her, her magic filling him and soothing him and more intense than she'd meant it to be. The Blackness fled with a thought and he sank slowly back onto the cold earth, breathing easier at the least.

She met his grey eyes staring up at her, unable to speak until he took the mask from her face, terrified he might not give her a chance to explain.

"Are you a ghost then?"

She shook her head.

"Then have I died and finally found you?" His fingers curled into her hair, pulling at the tresses, teasing her with the gentle tug. He shifted and touched the mask beneath her eyes and she was grateful for the dark of the moon that hid the blush she couldn't control, hid the changes in her appearance that she hated because she was not the woman he once knew, not anymore. "I'm not the same person either."

She blinked her eyes open, not having realized she'd closed them to his soft caress.

He brushed the lace once more, slipped his fingers beneath the soft edge and peeled the damp fabric from her skin.

"I don't understand."

She understood too much.

With a desire heightened by centuries of denial, she bent the few inches between them and claimed the kiss stolen from her by her brethren three hundred and eighty-eight years ago. She kissed him, and the Darkness answered her desire with a roaring rush of pleasure that consumed her, billowed out from her in great waves, caught him up in the maelstrom and bound them tighter into one being. Her heart did not just beat with him but was the same; his breath was hers, his flesh was a second skin and as sensitive as her own physical self. She was his memories as he was hers, her year spent as apprentice, trying to learn control of the dark power that she'd welcomed into her body to save his life, fighting to regain enough control that she was not swept away by the Night. The dreams he woke from, memories buried within his subconscious of pain upon pain, scars that bled against his psyche and echoed into his waking world. Months of relearning to breathe while his ribs healed and his lungs remembered that a deep breath didn't have to hurt. The pity in the eyes of the soldiers who had been there at his rescue, seen what had been done to the body. The pity from his king who saw only a broken son and could not reconcile the man who was and the one he had become. He brushed against the pain of her heart reaching for him only to be blocked by his conviction she was dead, the number of times her mother and the other elves stopped her from running to him, burned her letters, caged her in a cell surrounded by light that not even the Darkness filling her could overwhelm.

She leaned back first, looking down into eyes that she ached to stare into for whatever eternity waited for her. "I tried. I tried so hard to come to you. I begged her to send word, that you were dying from the not knowing, the pain worse than whatever tortures you'd suffered."

"I would not have believed anything but you standing before me." He brushed back the dark hair from her face, fallen forward around them at their kiss. "How? I thought she killed you."

"No. No, she said that the debt had been forgiven, only three lives bound my exile, the last was by your hand."

"But that's—"

"Her word is law, Kit. She said it and it was believed." She paused, answered his first question. How was she here now, if not then? "I woke in the temple and you were gone. You'd been gone for days. My mother sent you away with your guards, her healing as complete as she could manage, the body needing rest while the soul healed or fled. No one knew how to bring you back, and I was caught in the Void, unable to help even had I wanted." She did not resist touching his face, tracing the faint lines of magic that decorated his skin, the blessing of her mother and the other high priests of the Dienobolos. She laid her hand over his heart, felt the power of the Priestosolos that marked him.

It was an accident, that she let the surge of her magic fill her hand and flow into him. It was an accident, but she did not regret overwhelming her mother's binding and claiming him as hers alone.

"When I woke, the last of the light left me. My hair was black as the void, my eyes; my skin paled as a child of the Midnight must be pale. No matter if I sat in the light for hours, or chased the sun for days, it was like the bright rays could not touch me.

"I was so angry, Kit. I was so angry and so scared and any emotion, every emotion, threatened the little sanity I retained." She could not meet his gaze, afraid to see fear in them, disgust at what she'd become. "They were right to keep me locked away. And when I rose from the madness, I did not think you would want me any longer, had already let me go—"

"Never." He shifted and shifted again when she tried to pull away, holding her closer. "I will never let you go."

"I'm not the girl you knew."

"I'm not that man either."

He did not say that without her he was a shell. He did not need to say the words for she'd seen the truth when acting out her mother's final game, final test. That he'd threatened the priestess made her smile, enjoying that he'd loved her enough to avenge her against the highest ranking member of the Dienobolos.

"You never used to blush this much."

"I blushed," she could not help the small smile that came to her lips at his remark. "My skin just did not show it."

"It suits you, fair lady."

She did not fight his lead this time, allowing him to roll her to her back, smiling at the green stains that would rub into her dress with every kiss he gave her.

This one was a softer thing, born of joy and content, not laced with despair that the first might be the last as well. He kissed her, and her eyes closed, head tipping back as her staid prince, so proper for so very long, lost the battle she'd hoped to force him past all those years ago, so many times over the years.

He breathed against the pulse at her throat. "Your mother," he hesitated and she did not know where his thoughts had turned. "She said I was accepted. That I was for Iisforsos."

"The First to Touch the Stars. The first to walk amongst the Void and return with Its power, Its servant in this world."

He brushed the ridge of her brow, the corner of her eye, swept her lashed when she closed her lids to let him touch. "You.

She accepted me for you." His fingers were soft when they traced the swell of her lower lip. "Iisforsos."

Yes, that was what she was called. A new title for a new time just as she had come before him once bearing a different guise. But that was not what she wished him to call her. "That is not my name, Prince."

He rose over her, rose to stare down in her eyes. She wrapped her arms around his neck, holding him tight, waiting for long forgotten memories to emerge and to see the response she had once sought to deny.

He smiled, his weight and his warmth settling over her. "Then what is your name, my love?"

"Ella. Just Ella."

"No."

She frowned up at him, trying to read the deeper emotion within the smile in his eyes.

"Not 'Just Ella.'" He held her chin steady, leaned towards her until his lips brushed hers with his words. "My Ella. Always my Ella."

"My Prince. My Kit."

And it was true.

Epilogue

When the spring rains ended, there was a wedding.

It was not a small affair, as a prince's wedding cannot be small.

Nobles and knights, ladies fair and frail, all came for the final ball that the king would throw in honor of his son.

The streets of the city were filled with peasants and soldiers, with elves who left their wooden homes to visit those made of stone. There was smiling and crying, laughter and arguments and it was good and natural and in the end it was a type of magic, all the men and women and children gathered together in celebration.

In the month before the wedding, the prince and his captain rode through the city, rode the length and breadth of their kingdom. He spoke of the people, and she spoke of the land, and where they went they were received and they were accepted.

It is said that where the fair captain tread, health came. The sick healed. The old felt young again.

And where the prince followed, wisdom flowed. Men and women flocked to him for his counsel and his compassion.

The gates of the palace were thrown open for three days of feasting, and for three days there were no peasants or princes. Everyone danced and wined and dined as though they were equals sharing in their rulers' joy.

On the third night, as was tradition, the prince entered the ballroom and walked to his father's throne to sit upon the dais where he would someday rule.

He did not walk alone.

They sat on chairs pressed together, the prince and his captain, elegant, regal, and beloved of each other.

Prince Christophe de L'Avigne took his vows before a priest of Atha, his mother's patron goddess, the goddess closest to his father's heart. He took his vows before the Priestosolos of the Dienobolos, and offered his prayers to the Darkness. His captain held his hands, kneeling at his side to repeat the words back to him, binding the woods and the city into one, the gods of the light, and the Darkness combined.

It is said that she wore a dress as dark as midnight, studded with diamonds that sparkled in the light of the candles set to flame around her, that she brought with her the calming shadows of the woods and the quiet peace of a restful night. For her crown, a simple silver circlet bound up her dark locks, a jewel dripping atop her forehead, elegant, a thing of nature and of man.

The priest twined their wrists with a rope of ivy.

The priestess draped their shoulders with cloaks of fine wool woven barely a stone's throw from the palace steps in the city surrounded by stonewalls.

When the ceremony was over, and the multitudes held their breath to watch, it was the kiss shared, so pure and so sweet, filled with longing and with love, the love of lifetimes, that bound the two, bound the pain and the suffering and the salvation into one being, and promised a bright future.

And of course, the charming prince and his assassin princess lived…

Though Kit and his Captain have found their Happily Ever For-Now, *The Never Lands* have yet to accept the same fate.

Whose story is next?

www.AndiLawrencovna.com

A *Charming* Deleted Scene: *In the Still of the Night*

He woke with a breeze touching his warm skin, the kiss of cold rousing him from his fitful sleep.

His hand went to the knife beneath his pillow, eyes opened enough to scan the room before him and no more, unwilling to turn and alert whoever intruded into his sanctuary that he was aware of the threat. The cold was at his back, near the balcony and the glass doors that blocked him from the world. No sound came from that portion of the room, but assassins were silent as a general rule. Not that an assassin should have interest in him, beyond the normal reason of wanting to kill royalty. Silly really, to think that he survived the curse upon his head only to face the same threat for the rest of his life. He curled his fingers over the hilt, relaxing his muscles, prepared to turn at the first movement of another in his bed.

ଔ⁊ୠ

She stared up at him, her hands on his shoulders with his knife at her throat.

"I could have killed you."

"You could have tried." Her fingers traveled over his arm, down to his hand, loosening his grip on the blade, taking it from him, replacing it beneath the pillow rather than putting the knife beyond reach, beyond threat. She reached for him, running her fingers through his hair, pulling him down on top of her so that there was a subtle intimacy between them lacking from a moment prior. Her thumb brushed the dark circles beneath his eyes, traced the vein pounding in his forehead in time with his heart. "Talk to me, Kit."

It was not the whimsical question of the past, the desire to have a conversation, forget for a moment what was real around them. She wasn't asking for his history, or his dreams, or anything of the sort.

Her fingers passed over the grim lines at the corners of his mouth. "You're not sleeping, Love. You toss throughout the night. Stewards and guards say they hear screams coming from your rooms, but they can only guess at what terrors your dreams hold. Your father is worried about you. He set guards below your window and I think it's to catch you if you should jump." She caught his chin before he could look away, whether because his father thought him suicidal, or because his nightmares weren't as private as he thought. "You train but the men you train with are terrified for you—"

"Don't you mean 'of' me?"

Ella pinched his earlobe. "For you." Her fingers caressed the flesh she'd abused. "You've more control now than you ever had before on the field, but all that control is waiting for a spark to set fire to the anger inside you. You're wounded, and a wounded animal is the most dangerous."

A wounded animal. Wonderful. Just the type of descriptor he'd always hoped for, and to be called such by the woman he loved.

Kit snorted.

What next? Would she tell him he was damaged beyond repair? Discuss the scars that disfigured him head to foot? No, not head, never head. His tormentors had bruised and beaten him but never scarred his pretty face. Let there be something to identify him with, when they were done with him. Whip his arms. Burn his back. Cut his legs. Maybe take an appendage or two but they—

He scrambled away from her, not seeing the woman who was his heart and soul, but a face coming to maim him in the dark of a cell where there was no sunlight. His hand rose to ward her off, but she grabbed hold, kept him from falling from the bed.

The soft, comfortable bed, not concrete. His bed. His home.

Her wrist felt delicate beneath his harsh grip, his fingers no doubt leaving marks in her pale skin, but she didn't pull away or tell him to loosen his hold. She held him back, brought him back from the dark sludge of memory trying to drag him under.

Slowly, his breathing calmed. He saw her before his eyes, not some nameless face come to torment him. She shifted until she was kneeling before him, his back pressed to one of the bedposts, the velvet drapes surrounding him from behind while she braced him from the front.

There was no pity in her gaze. She did not stare at him like he was broken or needed coddling. Her hand gripped his, and he opened his arms so that she could move into his embrace, wrap him tight with her warmth, comfort him.

He tangled his fingers in her hair.

Her thumbs dug into his sides, the gaunt frame he managed to hide beneath layers of clothing revealed in his simple nightshirt.

He was still packed with muscle. Logically, he knew that more muscles wouldn't have saved him from being captured. His daily runs may have increased his stamina and speed, but he couldn't outrun an unseen arrow.

And of course, he knew what he would do the next time he was captured.

He'd use the arrow against himself.

But as she said, the guards were scared of him, "for" him. He almost prayed someone would attack, give him a reason to fight, to swing a sword without worry about the person meeting the exchange on the other side of the arc.

She pressed against the bulge of his ribs, the cut of muscles protecting them. Heat flowed from her hands, seeping through his skin and deeper into his tissues. The tension he hadn't realized knotted everything from his neck to his toes, eased and she'd only touched his sides. How had he forgotten that particular talent of hers? Of course, she didn't, hadn't, practiced it all that often on him, but still, he was grateful for it now.

"You're not eating—"

"I eat."

"Kit." One day returned to him and already he could hear the exasperation in her voice, that beautiful annoyance tinged with desire for more of what was once between them; the concern and care and something else voiced only the once, only hours ago, and held silent between them now, uncertain. "Do you keep any of it down?"

He snorted, hoping she couldn't see the blush on his cheeks, not wanting to admit to the weakness. "I eat."

And he had managed to keep his meal down tonight.

He had eaten something, he was sure. Hadn't he?

He didn't want to think about food.

Kit bent his forehead to hers, eyes closed to lean against her. His hands dropped to her waist, holding her in his embrace, reveling in the soft caress of her breath against the sweat dampened skin of his throat; nerves he didn't want to admit to jangled even knowing who she was before him.

He'd kissed her hand under his father's watchful gaze, the king's frown tinged with an upturn of lips.

Leon found them in the gardens, her white gown surrounding Kit where they laid on the ground, her hand pressed to his chest, his arms wrapped tight around her.

It had been a foregone conclusion that they would be married regardless of personal desires. That Leon had found Kit smiling at the to-be union was for the better. The king hadn't even yelled over impropriety this or that, though the old man had drawn a line at Kit returning to the palace with his wayward elfin betrothed alone and unchaperoned.

But that was then.

Gods, the changes a few hours wrought.

His father ensured that guards were posted at the princess-apparent's door, and that Kit made his way unmolested back to his own chambers, was locked safely away inside, alone.

Everything had been fine until he was back in his rooms, silent now that the ball was over, that most of the patrons had returned to what shelters they chose for the evening.

He put the fire in the grate out, pushed chairs in front of the grill so he wouldn't see the burning coals dying in the pit. It was warm enough outside. He had blankets if he needed more.

He hated fire, torches, candles, all of it. Rather the darkness, at least he couldn't see what was in store for him then.

He stripped off his court clothes, the scent of fresh grass lingering despite the stonewalls around him. It was easy to believe that she was real, that she wasn't a spell, when he was before her, easy to accept physical differences when she was in his arms and he could feel the truth of her beside him. But he'd had too many dreams of late where she was there, a fantasy gone when he woke.

"Tell me you're real, Ella. Make this more than a dream."

He didn't mean to say the words aloud. Every vision he'd ever had of her, the moment he asked if she was with him, it ended and he was alone.

He flinched when her hand dropped away from him, the gentle massage of her fingers through his hair left him wanting and aching and near insane thinking she was gone once more from him.

"Open your eyes, Prince."

A part of him expected to see reddish hair and emerald eyes staring at him, another piece expected a spectre.

The darkness that swirled in her gaze was unfamiliar and yet comforting all the same. "I'm here. I'm with you. There's no getting rid of me this time."

He almost smiled at the remark, knew she meant him to. "I've had visions of you before."

Her hands were touching him once more, running over his trembling arms, the chills tracking down his spine, making his teeth chatter though he wasn't cold. He was always cold.

She caught him when the post no longer sufficed to hold him upright, when his body curved into itself, a learned respond to the horrors he'd faced.

Why couldn't he escape them?

Why couldn't she force them away?

She helped him lower to the bed, pulled the covers back over his body, sweat and chills leaving him weak on the mattress. He slung an arm over his eyes, not wanting to see her, almost hoping she was another dream.

Had he been strong once? Was he so broken now?

He pushed her aside, flinging himself over the edge of the bed, hands scrambling for the pot beneath the dresser that he cleaned every morning before guard or servant came to fetch him. His stomach heaved, and, damn her, there was nothing there to come up, only bile that he pretended was not beset with the scent of iron.

It was one thing to suffer alone, another to fall prey to witnesses.

Her hand traveled the length of his spine, and he flinched from the touch even though her skin did not touch his.

With careful movements, she pulled the thick cotton shirt from his sweat dampened flesh, bared his scarred back to the darkness of his room. He didn't fight as she extracted his arms, raised the cloth over his head, let it drop beyond sight, or beyond his closed eyes, unwilling to look, acknowledge that she was looking at him.

How many times had he lied to himself, prayed, hoped she'd never see, never saw, his scars, knowing she'd been the one to find him in his hell all those months ago?

One arm dangled over the side of the bed, his head over-hanging the mattress, exhausted enough that he couldn't raise himself back to his pillows, letting her do as she would to him.

Softer than a butterfly's wing, the tips of her fingers trailed over lash marks, over burns, over scars made from nails scraping against his flesh, threatening the tumult in his stomach once more. He didn't remember most of those marks, not until he saw them, and even then the recollection was vague, hidden behind a mist only parted in his dreams. She traced the scars left by a mad man at the behest of his uncle. Then she traced the marks war had left on his skin: the lance broken through his cuirass reaching from hip to armpit; a sword that slashed a gash over his left shoulder and would have cut his spine had he not turned fast enough, too close to his throat for comfort, not close enough to end his life. Her touch moved over the scar of broken bone in his forearm from a fall from his bedroom on a midnight escape to the kitchens. His guards failed to catch him. Poor lads. The healer ensured the bone set straight, used magic to seal the skin, but the raised line remained as reminder of younger mistakes.

His head turned to the side, and she caressed up the line of his throat, the edge of his jaw, the nick where no stubble grew after the slice of a knife from an assassin's blade in the dark of night.

"My mother," she hesitated over the naming though her touch never left him. He found he didn't mind mention of the woman. The Priestosolos was a nonentity now that her daughter was returned to him. He nodded, and she continued like there had been no pause between them. "She bound the memories of the flesh behind a veil. I can sense it lingering beneath your skin." Her nails flicked over a round mark he knew came from a coal but couldn't remember the moment he gained the scar. "It should have faded by now, but you're fighting it, my mother's magic."

Kit heard the smile in her voice, wondered if his fight was a good thing or a bad thing, or if it was just that he was fighting her mother that caused her to smile.

"You shouldn't be able to deny her magic, but you've thwarted her for five hundred plus years. She should have known better than to spell you now."

"Should I not be fighting?" His words were hoarse, acid burned from his raw throat.

Her palm pressed to the middle of his back, fingers spread over as much of his skin that she could touch. "No, Kit, you shouldn't be fighting anymore."

And what would happen when he stopped?

But he didn't ask the question, having a good idea of the answer regardless of her words.

"I don't want to remember."

"My Kit." She laid against him, the catch of soft silk against his back sent different flutters through his stomach, less violent in their assault though no less intense. Her hand moved down his overhanging arm, and he let her draw it back to the bed, bent enough that their fingers laced together, pulled her closer into his body until it was her heart he felt beating in his chest.

"I don't mind the scars." What he meant was: he didn't mind the visible scars. There were worse that he couldn't see, that destroyed more than just the physical body he bore. He didn't want to bear those.

"It's time, Kit."

He didn't want to see, to remember. Rather the slow trickles invade his conscious than to tear the whole barrier aside and drown in the onslaught.

"Not an onslaught. Just removing the first bandages, a systematic uncovering until you're free of the nightmares, waking and not."

"There's no freedom from them, Ella."

"Would you rather the knowledge remain buried until something forces the memories to emerge? It could be a clap on the back. A handshake. A word. Who knows what will trigger the deluge you fear, but it will come, Kit. What happened won't stay buried forever. Better you should pull the bandage off at your own command than by another's accident."

He'd avoided it thus far. Mostly. Damnit.

He didn't want her to see them, the things he didn't want to remember, his response when those hidden truths were revealed.

"I already know, Kit."

He turned at that, turned and she fell away from him, rolled to her back so he could once more pin her to the mattress beneath his weight. "What?" Anger or terror, he wasn't sure, but his tone held more than a tinge of both as he stared down at her, this woman he loved and prayed didn't know his greatest shame.

"It's not shameful, Kit. You couldn't have done anything differently. Once captured, you were always going to suffer, and you saved others' lives in the taking; you didn't speak when they tried to break you."

"They fucking succeeded! I told them who I was. I told them I was the one they were looking for. Begged them to kill me, even if just to test the godsdamned theory. I didn't hold out against anything. The only salvation I could think of was that you—" *would never know.*

It wasn't the turning of his stomach that forced him from his bed this time.

He ignored the hand she reached towards him, moved without thought to the balcony doors, let the glass slam against the wall, not sure he would have cared if the panes broke with his actions as he bent over the railing trying to catch a breath restricted by broken ribs, by too tight flesh, by lungs unwilling to expand, filling with water and whatever else his body sought to kill him with.

Her arms wrapped around him, one hand placed over his heart, the other against his spine, pressing against his skin so that she was with him for every inhale, exhale.

"By the time you said you were the prince, they'd tortured you enough to know you would have said anything to end the torment. It wouldn't have mattered if you were speaking truth or lies; they just wanted to hurt you."

"Please stop."

"Kit."

"Please."

She obeyed, or acquiesced, or whatever. Her dark words stopped dredging up memories he'd rather leave buried, knowing she was right in bringing them to the front. Too many soldiers had come home from battles shell-shocked and battered, turned violent at the merest of touches because their psyches broke further beneath the strain of pretending they were all right.

Gods. She'd been the one to visit those poor men. Whether it was magic or simple compassion that calmed their souls, he didn't know, but they'd begun to heal with her touch.

He didn't want to have to face his past to reach that point.

"I lost control."

His head turned enough to see her standing at his side in the darkness.

A tendril of pitch unwound from the fabric of the universe around them, danced on an unseen breeze to the tapping of her fingers against his chest. She swirled her hands over his skin, and the darkness spun in waving patterns before his eyes. The thread split in three, wove together in a tight braid that she wound around his wrist, tattooed his skin with before drawing the magic from him, a line of heat remaining in its place across his flesh. She twined it like a garland through the rungs of the railing, and when he plucked at the shadow, it felt real and solid against his palm.

"I," he heard the hesitation in her voice, "did not have the best of control when I came for you. Emotions fray the best of sorcerers and I could feel your agony pulsing through my veins. It enraged me. I was lucky not to have killed one of our men with my hate." She stepped away from him, put an arms' length between their bodies. "Reaching between their conscious mind and their memories was easy. It was easy to pull the terrors they'd inflicted from their thoughts, to play out those visions within their heads, ensure they felt the pain they put you through even if their skin never broke because there was no whip or iron to touch their flesh. They felt it, everything they did to you, everything they planned on doing to you." She was the one shaking now, her arms wrapped tight around her chest, shadows obscuring her form from his sight though he knew she was within his reach. "I didn't want to stop. I tore their minds apart, committed the shells of their bodies to the Darkness and I felt nothing but justice from my actions. I did horrible things to those men. I said I did it for love, in my head I did it for love, but I had no control, no control and no conscious about destroying them for what they did to you, what they expected me to do.

"And then I found you and you tried to touch my cheek. And you died."

He'd never known the darkness to be so bright.

The ebony pools of her eyes stared at him from the midnight she'd drawn around herself, hid herself behind, a defense for when he shunned her same as he expected her to shun him for what he hadn't been able to control and had fought back from same as she.

She blinked.

He took the moment to cross the distance between them, pull her into his arms, press his lips to hers, still so new, this glorious touch between them. He pressed his lips to hers and knew the exchange was harsh and biting and there was little if any comfort in the action, but it was real. Pain was real. A pinch to pull yourself from a dream. How many times had he heard that throughout his life?

Her hands clenched his biceps, and he gentled his hold on her cheeks, fingers stroking, offering that same comfort she gave so easily.

"I'm evil."

"You're human."

She laughed, a harsh sound though a thread of humor pierced the darkness around them. "I'm an elf."

When he kissed her this time, it was a gentle exchange of breath, a nip, a sip, the taste of flesh meeting flesh. "You're a very human elf then."

"I told myself it was justice."

He tangled his fingers in her thick curls, only just realizing that most of her hair remained braided down her back, only the pieces disturbed by his touch broken free of the thick rope. The tie was easy enough to pull away, and he ensured that the heavy strands drifted from their binding. "Your magic, it comes from your belief in the Darkness, yes?"

She nodded against his hand, only his touch on her cheek displaying her actions, his eyes blinded by the shadows drawn tightly around her.

"Would your Darkness allow you to use it for vengeance if it was not righteously sought?"

"I don't know."

"Would your Darkness curse a babe fresh from the womb with the weight of the world on his shoulders?"

"Of course not. That would be—"

"Then I doubt It would allow you to taint Its power if It considered your actions unjust."

The two did not, exactly, equate, but that wasn't the point in the end.

He accepted her, all of her, the just and the unforgiving, the dark and the light.

She touched her hand to his heart, the darkness breaking away from her, returning her to his sight.

"Damn elf."

Her smile was tremulous. She was as broken as he.

"Why didn't you tell me? Why didn't you come to me?"

She shrugged, and he wiped the tear from her face. "I would have willingly offered my life for yours, Kit. To know you survived, to spare you what happened...I would have offered everything I was, I did offer everything I was." Her lips firmed in their smile. "I came back for you, but I had to learn control." She paused, and he found the silence comfortable between them despite the emotion. "I came as soon as I could."

"You should have come sooner."

"I know."

He held her gaze with his, stared into the starless sky of her eyes. "I don't want to remember."

"I know."

Kit didn't fight her as she led him back into his room, towards his bed. She ignored him when he tried to pull her from the side with his oft used bucket and the mess he'd already made of the night. When he remembered, would the damn panic attacks cease, or would he have to grow accustomed to them? He didn't ask, and she didn't offer an opinion. He tried to stop her from bending towards the copper tub, but the pot was engulfed in shadows, and when the darkness cleared there was no sign of the tumult of his stomach left behind. It was still mortifying to have her cleaning after him.

"You nursed me through food poisoning before."

He'd also been the one to poison her in the first place when he pulled the wrong mushroom for a stew and she'd managed to stop him before he took a bite but not in time to spare herself the ramifications.

"Consider us even now."

He accepted the balm to his pride that she offered, allowed her to replace the chamber pot beneath his side table, help him into the bed and beneath his covers once more. He watched from his place nestled in his pillows as she moved about his darkened room, ensuring his doors were locked, the balcony closed once more, shades drawn against the morning sunlight not far off if he had to guess. The darkness congregated around her, followed her from shadow to shadow as she moved. He heard the shuffling of logs arranged in the fireplace, the strike of a match and the hiss of lit timber. That his body tensed in expectation of the glow was not lost on him. That he relaxed when no light shown forth, only the gentle warmth of the fire brought to his side by her returning presence, did not go unnoticed either.

She returned, and his forehead furrowed.

"I was watching you. How did you—"

She crawled over the mattress to his side, his dress shirt from the earlier ball billowing around her shoulders until she settled with one arm over his chest, huffed and shifted until he extended an arm for her pillow and she relaxed into his side.

"Stop thinking, love. Sleep, just try to sleep, Kit. I won't leave your side."

"Until the guards—"

"Watch them try."

His laugh was cut in half by his yawn, his jaw popping as exhaustion finally took its toll. Nearly an entire year of sleepless nights. The lethargy he'd fought against for so long consumed him. Her words were a spell he didn't have the will to resist. The gentle caress of her skin against his, the quiet humming he hadn't realized she sang into the silence of the room, all of it lulled him towards whatever path she chose for him. He should fight the compulsion. He didn't want to.

Kit allowed the darkness of dreams to claim him.

ᨧᨵ

He woke to the soft press of lips against his, his hands curling around the arms bracketing his head, running over the satin skin beneath his palms. Sunlight streamed through the balcony door, the curtains pulled wide open now. It cast bright arcs of light across his room, across his bed, highlighting the auburn and green staring down at him. "You're using magic?"

Her lips curved up. "You shouldn't be able to tell."

"Your pupils are wide, Eli, too wide even if there's a circle of green around them." He brushed his thumb along her cheekbone. "And I've always known when you were using magic."

Her smile never faltered, but he noted the hardness of her gaze, the intensity with which she watched his face.

The colors bled slowly from her complexion, her hair. He found her changed visage calming to look upon. It was like, this new her, was someone different, someone who didn't need to know the horrors of their pasts even as she'd walked them with him.

He remembered the burns across his palms, across the soles of his feet. He hadn't told the bastard what he wanted to know, not when the man placed the pokers to his skin, maimed him and left him to the other prisoners' mercy. He'd fought, broken though he was. He remembered reaching into the fire grate, reaching for the red-hot ring glowing on the coals, clutching it to his palm while his fingers burned and his blistered flesh split, but he hadn't given it up easily. The guards had stomped on his hand, both hands. One of them had taken her ring. He didn't know what happened to it after that, but he'd tried to keep it. He'd fought for it, would bear the scar with pride, wouldn't let the memory cripple him.

She laid against his side, an arm reaching over his chest so that she could trace the circle on his palm. "What was it of?"

"A ring." He watched her face carefully, her black eyes, the midnight hair. "I was going to give it to you the last night of the ball."

Her gaze turned up to his, a blush rising to her cheeks.

"Would you have said yes, Ella?"

Her fingers curled around his, raised his arm and pulled him towards her until they were both on their sides facing each other. She brought his hand to her lips and kissed the burnt skin, white with scars, kissed the ring he'd lost. "I never needed a ring, Kit." Her blush deepened, and he stared until she looked away.

"What? What aren't you telling me?" He couldn't help the note of teasing in his voice, not when she blushed to prettily and hid so ineffectually against him.

"I knew I was an idiot when we rode through the palace gates that first night after the ball." She looked up at him from half-closed eyes, doing her best to hide what emotion lingered within. "I would have chosen you, if you'd asked me again after my brethren attacked. Captain or wife…I would have chosen you."

"You did."

"You know what I mean."

He laughed, let her move his hand where she would, his fingers trailing down her cheek, her throat, settling over her heart. Yes, he knew what she meant. "Better to have waited four hundred years."

"Liar." She shifted closer into his chest, using his bent elbow as a pillow to rest against. Her eyes closed, and he stroked along her side, watching her doze, only then realizing that she didn't flinch from his scars, from the rough brush of his skin against hers. That he didn't flinch at her touch, physically or mentally.

He could feel the memories within his head, but they weren't rushing to bombard him. They had a cognizance of their own, waiting patiently until he was ready to address them, no longer fighting against the veil pulled over his mind, his conscious no longer beating them back.

He should be worried about a servant or guard coming to check on them, seeing the mess that was his body, the woman in his arms, but he couldn't bring himself to care with her there with him. He was at peace. He wasn't worried whether she was a dream or not beside him, content with his reality as it was.

His stomach grumbled, and she smiled against his chest, no more asleep than he.

"Evil elfling."

She laughed but didn't move, and he listened to the hungry growls of his body. Hells, he actually enjoyed the sensation of being hungry after so long hating the thought of food and its inevitable reemergence. He was looking forward to having a meal for the first time in recent memory, not having to choke down what his father placed before him.

"If you give me a few more hours of sleep, prince, I'll make sure you have all of your favorites for supper tonight. I'll even cook if you'll make your stomach stop that damn awful noise."

"Weren't you the one telling me I should eat more?"

"At respectable hours of the day. Sunrise not being one of those times."

It was good to laugh, to feel the joy of the emotion as it blossomed in his chest, didn't hurt or drag up visions of suffering. It wasn't the crazed laughter of the tower. His breath caught at the thought, but there was no flood of memory, no fear of truths it would reveal.

The fear would return, he was sure of that. She'd said he wasn't free of the nightmares yet. But for now, for once, he acknowledged that they weren't the end of his world, just an un-wished for beginning, something to overcome and move beyond as time passed.

He kissed her forehead, "Don't magic me asleep again, Witch."

"I un-magiced you, Prince."

"I suppose that's alright then."

She shifted closer to him, and he closed his eyes, thought happy thoughts with her by his side.

Appendices
Appendix 1
The Lands of Shcew

It is quite the thing to close your eyes and wake in another time, in another place, in another land so very unlike your own that it is both wonderful and terrifying in turn.

Herein lies that which I have learned so far on my journeys to the Never Lands. Though I've yet to learn a great deal of the lands themselves, what I have been able to piece together is fascinating. From Kingdoms of giants to dead islands burned clean with dragon fire, the Lands are fascinating.

I suppose, to begin, it would be appropriate to start with the planet's name. As you can imagine, a land so unlike our own and yet infinitely similar could rightly be called "Earth." In truth, they term the ground they walk on as such, but the planet itself has quite a different appellation.

Shcew.

Shcew received its name from the first bird that landed on the lands. There is a complicated history to which I was not privy. The basics of the story that I heard was that after the initial land masses formed, the world was dormant of life, waiting to be inhabited. The gods who created the planet, though this may well be only one creation story of the land, waited and watched and finally, from out of the dark wastes of their universe, a tiny bird, the closest approximation I can think of would be our sparrow, slipped through the atmosphere and settled on a small piece of earth at the top of their planet, laid its head upon the ground, and slept. It spread its wings wide, and sprawled its legs out, and from its body sprang the land of Prutwl, the great crown at the head of their world.

But that was only one myth, and who is to say if it is true or not?

The planet itself consists of six land masses. Some historians divide the southernmost continent into two distinct continents, but once upon a time, the lands were connected by a bridge and were as one.

Below is a brief history of each mass as I've learned so far. Most of my time has been spent in Lornai, predominantly in Spinick itself, so please forgive any misrepresentations as I've not the skills of a natural historian or geographer and have done the best I could.

Prutwl

The northernmost continent consists of a string of peninsulas circled together, vaguely resembling a large crown that might once have been worn by the world. Covered in snow and ice for twelve of the nineteen month year, Prutwl is home to the first races, those born of the elements when Shcew was created in the cosmos.

Though it is home to the elements, the land itself is bereft of magic, its people resenting the unnatural aspects of their brethren from other lands.

There is speculation that the animosity between magic and non-magic folk began when select rogue priests demanded sacrifice from the people of Prutwl, and rather than allowing their sons and daughters to be killed, they rose up and forced the wizards and witches and false-gods, from the land and have kept it bereft of magic since. Those who possess even the slightest of magical talents are exiled, if not worse, according to myth.

Kirbi

A desert continent riddled with hidden oases of lush rain forests and barren subterranean villages. Most of the inhabitants live beneath the sands and rarely walk above ground. Those who do make their homes in the rain forests battle Manticore and Yateveo for supremacy. The Djinn are a hidden race, building their habitats deep within the jungles, concealed by the trees. The few trading ports on the outskirts of the continent discourage explorers though the riches found in the land tempt foreigners to overstay their welcome.

Zephra

Known as the vanishing isle, Zephra was once the most lush and beautiful of all the Never Lands. During the Third Age, the great dragons who made the island their home were betrayed by the humans who shared the island with them, the Miestians. The War of the Dragons raged for nearly fifteen hundred years before the dragons, fearing defeat, set the entire island on fire, killing all the inhabitants, flora, fauna, and human alike. With the destruction of the island, the dragons were said to have sank into the ash of their homeland and fallen asleep, waiting for the next attack to come against them.

The island itself is thought to be more myth than truth as it is an untethered land mass and moves with the tides through the oceans. Those who see the island rarely live long enough to report back to anyone on its whereabouts, and its name is spoken in hushed whispers, as legend says that simply stringing the syllables together will call down the fiery wrath of the serpents who sleep there.

Wen

A series of island connected by bridges makes up the continent of Wen. The bridges were built by the first races as each of the five islands is the home of the elements of Shcew. The largest of the islands, Eao, is the birthplace of earth and the birthplace of man. Arising from the dust, man was made from water and air and given legs to walk and arms to build, or so goes the ancient myth. I'Che is the land of water. Sool dedicates its soil to the breath of air that wraps around its great mountain. Lars is the furthest south of the equator and, as the hottest island in the chain, is a celebrant of fire. Roa Shar holds the great temple of Shcew and worships the light that bathes the world, and the dark that shelters it in slumber. It is dedicated to spirit, and learning to be one with the body and the earth.

Istar Ahn and Ohn

Twin continents at the southern pole. The lands were once connected by a strip of land called the Vein. When the bridge was destroyed, the lands separated into different entities in entirety. Istar refuses to allow visitors to their shores and trading was embargoed during the Second Golden Age.

Lornai

As the second largest continent on the planet, Lornai was once one nation but the *War that Ended the First Golden Age* saw the land split into nine independent kingdoms. Though small skirmishes still occur, the land is at general peace with the Northern Kingdoms of Drewes, Quifol, and Faoust bordered by mountains and the Middle Kingdoms separated by the Great Forest of Dienobo and its elven protectors, the Dienobolos. The Southern Kingdom of Spinick, the Great Walled City, was once the capital of the land, and still boasts the greatest resources on the continent. At the end of the Great War, the Gods foretold that a son would be born to the King of the City during the rise of the Fourth Age and with his birth, the Land would either rise above itself or it would fall into the oceans. The full prophecy was lost long ago, though theories run rampant as to its origin throughout the kingdoms.

Appendix 2
The Calendar of the Never Lands

The planet of Shcew rotates on a thirty-two hour cycle. As with our world, they revolve around a sun at the center of their solar system. Because of their sun's enormity, and their relative size and rotational speed, one solar year for the planet lasts six hundred and twenty days. A leap year occurs every seven cycles, increasing the length of the year to six hundred and twenty two days.

The year is divided into nineteen months with eight day weeks. In opposition to our own yearly cycle, their New Year begins in the middle of their Summer. Though the day changes yearly, the month of V'Roshar hosts the Longest Day, a celebration of the Light of the World. As is custom, the Longest Day is a day of festival where upon great parties are held and torches are lit throughout the night to keep the sun shining for the thirty-two hours.

In contrast, Rashel, the mid-winter month, celebrates the Day of Night, the longest night of the year. A more sober celebration, the Worshippers of the Darkness hold silent vigils on this Night, fare-welling their dead, adjudicating grave crimes, remembering that from the dark we came and to the dark we must return. For others outside of the Darkness, the day is for family, often commencing with great parties that last until the dawn of the next morning.

The days of the week are as follows:

The First Day of the week is a day of rest on the continent of Lornai. Though the world follows the same structural month and date pattern, cultures change what each day is representative of. For example, in Kirbi, Timresiet is a day of religion. Vendors close down their shops and are expected to present themselves at their known houses of worship. Kirbi is a rather religious continent, as they have little else to unify them with. It is another reason outsiders are mistrusted and denied entry into the land. In Lornai, Spinick specifically, Timresiet is a day typified as a bathing day. Public bath houses open early and close late so that men and women can make use of the provided water to bathe in. Though other shops and stalls are open on this day, it is considered a day of light work and general rest.

Seventh and Eighth days are also days of rest, though many people choose to work on Parlquoet, Eighth Day, so as to prepare for the upcoming week. Parlquoet is also a day of religion in Lornai, though customs vary by kingdom.

Second through Sixth days are work days. The typical vendor opens his or her shop an hour after sunrise. The hour before is for setting up stalls since, at least in Spinick, the streets are required to be cleared on Timresiet as and per royal decree. Vendors are allowed to remain at their store fronts and shops until an hour after sunset, the curfew in place for their and their monarchy's protection. Outside of the city proper, such strict protocol is not enforced, though those towns are subject to their own laws and guidelines.

In contrast to Spinick, the Dienobolos observe no weekly rest days, all eight spent working at something or another. They do, however, celebrate the Dark of the Moon as a three day stretch of the month wherein obligations are foregone for relaxation and meditation.

First Day:	Timresiet
Second Day:	Onoui
Third Day:	Vernoui
Fourth Day:	Saioui
Fifth Day:	Oweloui
Sixth Day:	Moui
Seventh Day:	Samseiet
Eighth Day:	Parlquoet

Appendix 3
A Closer Look at <u>Lornai</u>

The Elves of the **Dienobo** were the first settlers of the land. As an immortal race, they knew the importance of ensuring the wellbeing of their homeland. They cultivated the earth, nurtured the trees, found ways to coexist within the forests that once covered the continent proper. It was not until after the *Great War* that the Dienobolos took up swords to defend their homes. By then, most of the continent had been conquered, the land stripped of forests, barren but for what was required to feed and build for the people. The elves hated the destruction of their continent, became warriors unparalleled among the races of the land. It was during the *Third Age* that they were relegated to their small remaining forested home. Upon threat of fire, ultimate destruction of all they knew, the Night Folk retreated to their forests, swearing peace unless their homes were invaded and then swift vengeance upon those who would dare their retribution.

Of **Traimktor** little is known even with their close proximity to the woods of the Dienobo. Rumor has it that the inhabitants of the Forbidden Realm were once elves. Beyond that truth, suspicion only. Some say that the men and women of Traimktor were so disgusted with the people of the land, their own kind included, they fled to the small kingdom and refused to leave for any reason, no contact with the world outside their own community. Even the elves that were once kin were forbidden the stolen land. Another myth is that the inhabitants of the small country were once elves, cursed to live alone, too violent even for the warriors of the wood to control. They were cursed to live like beasts as penance for the lives they had taken during the wars, cursed until they relearned their humanity. Whether they are immortal as their brethren or short lived like the beastly forms they inhabit, it is unknown. But on quiet nights, if you listen carefully, you can hear the call of the wolves and the bears, griffin and wyvern deep within the trees.

During the first age, other races began to venture into the land. The once fertile lands of the south grew fallow, only the harshest, sturdiest of vegetation surviving as their caretakers failed to upkeep the earth. The Men of **Quifol** were a solitary people, a warring people. They held to the southern tip of the land, fighting back invaders though they seldom ventured past their own borders despite their deadly tendencies. Most of what is known of their land is speculation. The kings, leaders, of the grassland folk do not engage in trade among the other lands of their continent. They are considered a closed territory. Some say that there was a time when the Men of cQuic did leave their grasslands. Stories of young daughters going missing from playing in the fields, little misses disappearing from their beds at night, run rampant along the border of the land. The last story was told long ago, but Quifol's neighbors lock their doors at night, place totems outside their houses to keep the foreign men from their children.

Trolls do not take kindly to the abduction of their kin, male or female. As a mortal race, their lives ranging less than one hundred years, their children are their only source of immortality to them. The Faoustians fight hard to keep their land and families safe. Amusingly, as a short lived race, they do not fear death or battle, often plying their trade as swords for hire. Then again, when they are surrounded on all sides by battle hardened countries like Quifol and Gouldaria, the citizens of *Faoust* require hardy sword arms to protect themselves.

Following accordingly then, *Gouldaria* separates Drewes and Faoust. The dwarves, vicious, ruthless creatures that they are, are limited in the land they can conquer by the mountains that surround them and the fierce nations at their sides. Despite their bloodthirsty tendencies, the dwarves, as well as being trained soldiers, are skilled craftsmen and armorers. Perhaps their greatest despondency comes from sitting before their forges creating great swords to swing at their enemies, and their enemies being too strong to attack.

Thankfully, the mountains keep the dwarves from **Drewes**. Though the giants are a larger race, as mortal as their dwarfish neighbors, they are a gentle people. They are slow to anger, and slower still to war. Understandably, no nation wishes to provoke the large folk, though they've shown no tendency towards brutality throughout their long tenure as caretakers of the mountains.

Of **Mrgloth** there is nothing known. The land is steeped in magic but who can say aught else? The sand that blows from the land is heavy with gold. Beyond that, nothing. All who have tried to breach their borders have died, bodies found broken and bloody, thrown to the rocks before ever reaching what lies beyond the giant hills. The first to forge a path to the nation will be hailed a hero, or die unheard from again.

Thankfully, the dragon shifters of **Arqueania** are a more tractable group. They trade openly, magic freely, live peacefully with their neighboring lands. Though fire runs rampant through their veins, making their dispositions quick and dangerous to displease, the men and women themselves are quite amiable, though a sadness lurks beneath their smiles. Whether they miss their kin from Zephra, or are kin at all, is unclear. But they've proven wise counsel and fair judges, swift to action and equally swift to penance when it is required. Then again, for a species that lives near unto five thousand years, many arguments could occur throughout a lifetime, and when tempers are so volatile, apologizing is a skill best learned young.

What, then, can be said of the humans? Of all the races of the lands, the residents of *Spinick*, the Great Walled city, are, perhaps, the least impressive of the lot. Engineers, pioneers, bastards and kings, the populace is a strange hodgepodge of the best and worst of the peoples of Lornai. Their first ruler was elected to the position. His kin have reigned justly ever since. They are the sons and daughters of the Gods, favored to be called the Heavenly Hosts children though little truth in the saying remains. Still, they must be blessed by some higher power, for they have never failed a test, always rose to a challenge, have defeated all and sundry sent against them and reigned as the mightiest of the kingdoms of Lornai though they are one of the smaller lands. Immortals too, magical, in part, the humans of Spinick are a mystery that is accepted as normal and unquestioned by the world.

Appendix 4
The Religions of Lornai

Dienobo: *Worshippers of the Darkness*

Since the beginning of time, there has been Darkness. From the ethos, came a great clap and into that Darkness was born life. Life grew and formed there, and with it there was peace. But light intruded, touched the children of the Night and bathed the ground they walked upon in brilliance, opening their eyes to a world unseen beneath a blanket of Ebony.

The Darkness allowed the light to shine, for even though the heavens were bright, they fell to Shadow in the end.

From the Night stepped forth aspects of the dark.

Pirie, the Lord of the Lit Path, the Master of the Void. To Him all prayers are heard and from Him all prayers are answered. The Priests of the Darkness were given the grave task of creating law for those who took solace in Shadow.

The ***Liaea***, the Inner Blackness of the Body, that which is Born from the Dark Womb and Returns to the Ebony Grave. Healers, teachers, those who dedicated themselves to the welfare of others kneel before the Body of Night given name.

The Master of the Final Midnight, *Echi*, the Lord of Death, the Father of New Life. One cannot come without the Other. Judge and jury, the dedicants of Echi grant mercy, ensure repayment of the debt, protect the Shadows even unto the Blackness of their own souls.

Rouchim of the Earth, the Keeper of Secrets, the Lady of the Hallow Ground and Sacred Tree. They who till the earth, work within the dirt, wander the paths between trees, tread where four and two footed brethren run, worship all those creatures living under the Night's Same Sky and offer thanks to the Darkness for the gifts grown in black places pay homage to the Dark Mistress.

Ashet, the Laborer, the Sentinel, the Lord of the Forge. Those who worship the art of life, from crafting shelters to guard the dreams of their people, to building boats to cross the waters that reflect back the light of the stars shining from the Void, give their love to the Lord who levels and remakes the world.

The Worshippers of the Darkness bear an affinity for the earth and all its natural creations. They draw strength and magic from the Night itself, walk dreams and darkened pathways too shadowed to invite others onto the road to new life.

Children of the Gods

Herein worship to the Gods.
Look to them for your Salvation.

Surprisingly, the polytheistic religion of Schew trends towards our traditional understanding of Greek Mythology with a hierarchy of gods to whom one should pray depending on circumstances. The general belief is that each person can associate with one or two of the primary gods whom they offer sacrifices to as their personal totems, honoring all the gods as a whole but with emphasis on their personal choices.

Like the Dienobolos, the religion is separated by aspect. For instance, *Atha* is the Goddess of Warfare and Justice, much like what the Greek Athena would have been known for. She also combines the religious beliefs of Artemis and Aphrodite as the patron Goddess for young women in love, the hunters and warriors, soldiers, and judges throughout the land.

Sei is representative of the natural world, both land and sea. He is as much the patron of the sailor as he is the farmer. Compared to our mythological references, he could be considered an amalgamation of Poseidon, Demeter, and Hephaestus. Considered a god of creation, he is given right of rule over craftsmen and artists as well.

Zeus, contrary to our foundation in myth, is a minor god of nature, in particular of the animals that run and fly. As a shape changing colossus, farmers, whose trade is in livestock, worship him. With sacrifice, it is said that Zeus will descend to the earthly plane of existence and seed both mare and heifer, increasing the quality of the livestock with his heavenly offspring.

The mightiest of the gods then is *Hades*, known as the Lord of Life. With the power over both the living and the dead, Hades rules the other gods of the pantheon, both as father and judge for all those under his care. Similar to our mythos, Hell remains a place of damnation of the spirit though they have no concept of "heaven" as we understand it. Since the Children of the Gods are mostly those of the immortal races, when Death does come for them, they are seeking the oblivion of the void rather than resurrection or continued existence elsewhere. Hell then is where those sentenced to "live on" go to suffer, complete with fire and brimstone.

End Notes:

The Gods are more myth than actual evidence to the people who worship them. Never having walked on the lands of Shcew, the gods are a distant faith to believe in. Since there is no origin story associated with the mythology, and since I seemed familiar enough with the religion itself, I speculate that I am not the first to cross from our world to theirs, and, as humans are like to do, those ancestors of mine who made the transition brought with them their own faiths and beliefs which were then incorporated within the world they lived in.

I should mention that, as a newer religion in the scheme of Shcew, the Gods are widely popular amongst evolving races as something to strive towards, as well as being looked down upon by other religions, such as the Dienobo, who discredit the beliefs of anyone else. To be fair, discredit is the incorrect term. The Dienobo are quite willing to believe that there are beings powerful enough to interact with the world on a creational basis, with the understanding that these beings are minor "gods" compared to the Darkness whom they worship.

As I have yet to explore more of the world than my brief stay has allowed, I expect I will be supplementing my appendices as I gain more information, so please bear with me as I go along.

Appendix 5
A Brief Pronunciation Guide

For simplicity's sake, I have used the Common Tongue of Lornai as the basis of pronunciation for the days of the week and months of the year below. The Dienobolos have a language of their own which I have done my best to spell phonetically throughout the narrative. Only basic translations exist of their tongue.

BASIC PRONUNCIATION GUIDE: COMMON TONGUE OF LORNAI		
WORD	**IPA PRONUNCIATION**	**PHONETIC PRONUNCIATION**
Months of the Year		
V'Roshar	vr - ouʃ - ɑːr	**vr**oom-**oce**an-**shar**d
Tippum	taɪp - ɛm	**type**-vell**um**
Dellum	diːl - ɛm	**deal**- vell**um**
Genlum	dʒen - lɛm	**gen**tle- vell**um**
Brumm	bruːm	**broom**
Yyxum	jaɪks - ɛm	**yikes**- vell**um**
Yuaar	hɪə(r)	**you-are**
Neise	Nis	**niece**
Quaar	kweɪ - ər	**quake-are**
Rashel	retʃəl	**rate-shell**
Pereshel	perɪ -ʃəl	**peri**sh-**shell**
Mishel	mɪt -ʃəl	**michelle**
Apshel	eɪp -ʃəl	**ape-shell**

Frenshel	fri:n -ʃəl	**f-preen-shell**
Harshel	hær -ʃəl	**hair-shell**
Cresch	kræ –sch	**crash-shell**
Wipshel	waɪp -ʃəl	**wipe-shell**
Linkshel	lɪŋk -ʃəl	**link-shell**
Vellim	vel -i:m	**v-fell-seem**
Days of the Week		
First Day: Timresiet	taɪm ri:ˈs ɪt	**Time-reset**
Second Day: Onoui	ɑ:n wi:	**on-Ouija**
Third Day: Vernoui	vərˈn wi:	**vernacular-Ouija**
Fourth Day: Saioui	saɪ wi:	**sigh-Ouija**
Fifth Day: Oweloui	aʊl wi:	**owl-Ouija**
Sixth Day: Moui	em wi:	**m-Ouija**
Seventh Day: Sam-seiet	sʌˈm si: ɪt	**sam-sight-et**
Eighth Day: Parlquoet	pɑ:lə - kwə ɪt	**parliament-quote-et**
The Never Lands		
Prutwl	pru:-tu:l	**prudence-tulle**
Kirbi	kɜ:rb-bi:	**Curb-bee**
Zephra	z-ef-r-ɑ:	**z-eff-r-ah**
Wen	wen	**when**
Lornai	lɔ:r-naɪ	**lore-nigh**
Istar Ohn	ɪztɑ:r oʊ-n	**Is-tar ohm-n**
Istar Ahn	ɪztɑ:r ɑ:n	**Is-tar khan**

Shcew	ʃuː	**shoe**
Lornai		
Dienobo	deɪ-ɪn-əʊbəʊ	**Dee-en-oboe**
Traimktor	treɪ-m-k-tɔːr	**train**-m-k-**tor**
Quifol	kwɑːˈf- l	**coif**fure-waf**fle**
Faoust	faʊst	**faust**
Gouldaria	guːl-dæ(r)iə	**gul**ag-**dahl**(**r**)**ia**
Drewes	druː es	**drew-s**
Mrgloth	mɜː(r)g-ləʊθ	**myrrh-g-loth**
Arqueania	ɑːk- keɪn- iə	**ark-cane-ia**
Spinick	spɪnɪk	**spinick**
Religions: Dienobo		
Dienobo	deɪ-ɪn-əʊbəʊ	**Dee-en-oboe**
Pirie	paɪ-riː	**pie-rea**ch
Liaea	laɪ-ə-ɑ	**Lie-a-ah**
Echi	eʃə	**ech**elon
Rouchim	ruːeɪ-ʃəˈm	**roué-chem**ise
Ashet	æʃ ɪt	**ash-et**
Religions: the Gods		
Atha	ɑːð- ɑː	**fath**er-**ah**
Sei	saɪ	**si**ze
Zeus	zuː es	**Zeus**
Hades	heɪdiːz	**Hades**

About the Author

Andi Lawrencovna lives in a small town in Northeast Ohio where she was born and raised. After completing her Masters in Creative Writing, she decided that it was time to let a little fantasy rule her life for a while. *The Never Lands* were born out of a frustration with happily-ever-afters, and a burning desire for the same.

For more information on Andi and *The Never Lands*:

www.AndiLawrencovna.com

Made in the USA
San Bernardino, CA
10 April 2016